eternal
BONDS

eternal
BONDS

Manoj Singh

Published by
Rupa Publications India Pvt. Ltd 2013
7/16, Ansari Road, Daryaganj
New Delhi 110002

Sales centres:
Allahabad Bengaluru Chennai
Hyderabad Jaipur Kathmandu
Kolkata Mumbai

ISBN: 978-81-291-2489-0

10 9 8 7 6 5 4 3 2 1

In the memory of my dear mother, Smt. Krishna Singh.

◆

Dedicated to all the innocent children who spend their childhood in an environment of repression.

Section 1

1

ADITI looked at the clock on the wall opposite her with half-open eyes and saw that it was 11 p.m. Yet again, she had gone to bed waiting for Amit. Before sleep overtook her again, the railway PBX phone rang in all its shrillness.

Her eyes flew open—she assumed it would be Amit on the other end. He would be looking for an excuse to explain why he had not come in today. Too tired to sit up, she remained lying down as she picked up the receiver of the phone and said softly, 'Hello…'

'This…this is Dr Amit Saxena's daughter. May I know who's speaking?' the voice on the other end sounded agitated.

'Beta, this is Aditi Aunty.'

'Aditi Aunty!'

Alert and awake by now, Aditi sat up.

'Aunty, please come to our house immediately. Papa has collapsed in the bathroom after he said he had a severe pain in his chest. He was trying to vomit. He even called out to me. He was trying to say something but collapsed at the door before he could speak…' Akanksha's words burst out in a single breath as she sobbed.

'Where is your mother, beta?' Aditi asked, forcing herself to remain calm.

'Mummy…well…Aunty, please come home first…' Saying this, Akanksha hung up without completing her sentence.

Aditi felt she was in the throes of a nightmare. She got up in a hurry and her hands automatically went to the call bell near her bed. Immediately after ringing the bell, she picked up her bag and packed in important injections, medicines and her sphygmomanometer. She hurriedly picked up her stethoscope before leaving the room and rushed to the door without waiting for a ward boy or a nurse. Her brain was completely active by now, but she could not understand what had happened to Amit.

'This is definitely an emergency. It must have been cardiac pain, could even be MI... myocardial infarction,' she thought to herself. As she stepped out, she met the nurse on duty who was walking quickly towards her in response to the bell.

'Yes, madam!'

'Sister, call the ambulance driver—I am going to Dr Amit Saxena's place and I want you to reach his house along with a ward boy. I think Doctor Sahib has had severe cardiac pain. It could even be MI. He has fallen unconscious. Keep essential first-aid and an ECG machine with you. Check the oxygen in the ambulance...' Aditi headed towards her car while giving instructions.

The verandah was deserted. On reaching the parking lot, she saw the ambulance there but the driver was nowhere near it. 'Must be sleeping somewhere nearby,' she thought as she got into her car quickly and drove towards the hospital's huge iron gate. It was open and as she drove out of the compound, she saw that the market was closed and the streets were deserted because it was late in the night and slightly cold. She crossed Indira Market and the railway bridge, driving fast towards Amit's house. Questions were rising in her mind at the same pace at which the car was moving and she was trying to find answers to them. She had observed that Amit had fallen very quiet in the past few days and looked sad most of the time, almost as if he'd lost the will to live. Life seemed to have become a burden for him. At times, she could smell alcohol on his breath even during the day. She had tried to stop him several times, trying to use her influence on him. She had even promised to look after him forever... What had happened? Was it all because of Nikita? She could not make sense of anything. She was so immersed in her thoughts that she did not even realize she had reached Amit's place. He lived in one of the railway bungalows quite close to the hospital.

She saw Aniruddh was waiting for her, sitting on a chair outside the garden. When she drove into the compound, Aniruddh came running behind the car, saying, 'Aunty, come fast!'

Aditi had just stepped out and closed the door of the car when she saw Akanksha rushing towards her. She took her bag and ran towards Amit's bedroom but Akanksha signalled to the room at the other end of the house. As Aditi reached the other bedroom, she saw Amit sprawled on the floor close to the door that led to the bathroom from the bedroom.

She kept her bag on the bed and sitting on the floor, immediately placed Amit's head on her lap while checking his pulse. It was weak but his heart was beating. He was unconscious, his eyes half open and his mouth frothing. She rubbed his chest and after cleaning his mouth, tried to give him oral resuscitation. Even before the ward boys and nurses arrived, she placed Amit's head in Akanksha's lap, took a syringe out and started looking for Amit's vein to administer an intravenous enzyme. Amit lay limp, like a tree that had not been watered for years. She was finding it difficult to find the vein as his blood pressure had dipped considerably.

Aditi drew in a deep breath and told Aniruddh, 'Come, let's make your father lie on the bed.'

Aniruddh, who was a sixteen-year-old boy, was observing Aditi with wide, worried eyes. He helped Aditi and Akanksha put Amit on the bed. Aditi placed an aspirin tablet on Amit's tongue, then looked around and saw that this was the children's room. There were two tables with books scattered all over—it seemed that they spent a lot of time studying. But then she felt that Amit's life, his happiness and grief, were limited to this room. If there were posters of favourite heroes and heroines on one wall, several posters of great leaders and philosophers adorned the facing one. The inspiring quotes on the wall were enough to touch one's heart. Clothes were strewn on the bed and shoes lay in disarray on the floor. While Aditi looked around, she massaged Amit's chest gently and was constantly checking her watch, anxiously waiting for the ambulance.

When she heard the ambulance arrive, she saw Aniruddh running in with the ward boy holding the stretcher. Without losing any time, they hoisted Amit onto the stretcher and ran to the ambulance. Aditi and Akanksha sat next to Amit in the ambulance. Aniruddh stood in the verandah, his face creased with worry as the ambulance left the bungalow.

Akanksha looked back at the house receding in the distance and then looked at her father. She asked Aditi, crying, 'Aunty, what is wrong with Papa? Will everything be fine?'

'Everything is all right, there is no need to worry,' Aditi said, taking Akanksha's hands in her own to reassure her.

In a few minutes, Amit was in the special room of the ICU. After wearing the oxygen mask, Aditi asked the nurse to put the ECG machine on and checked his blood pressure—his condition was precarious. The ECG showed that Amit had suffered a strong myocardial infarction, a high-intensity heart attack. Therefore, Aditi mixed morphine and nitroglycerin into the glucose drip. She knew that the next four to six hours were crucial. As half an hour passed, several thoughts gripped her. She had not left Amit's side for even a minute, stroking his forehead with love. But Amit was still unconscious, unaware of her loving touch. Akanksha was standing next to her father with tears in her eyes—she didn't know what to do.

Before she called Dr Khurana, the senior heart specialist, Aditi gently raised Amit's eyelids and looked into his eyes—and saw that even though he was unconscious, his eyes seemed to convey a message; he seemed to be struggling to communicate.

2

ANIRUDDH had started knocking at the door to wake Ma up the moment the ambulance had left. Ma had fought with Papa again this evening. He would often get irritated with his father's habit of not reacting to what Ma was saying. He loved his mother, but he resented his father's silence even when her behaviour was unacceptable. He failed to understand why. He wanted Papa to be harsh with Ma at times and today he had hated the fact that Papa had remained quiet, not responding even when Ma was shouting. Her anger would rise steadily and she would calm down on her own. But today, one sentence of Papa's, 'Okay, you are getting tired now. Go to sleep…' had made Ma extremely angry and she had shouted at him, saying, 'Yes, of course, that is what you want, that I go to sleep forever…'

And then, Ma had taken a lot of sleeping pills. Papa was trying to stop her from doing so when Aniruddh saw her pushing him out of the door. Then she locked it from inside. Papa had knocked hard at it saying, 'Nikita, I am sorry. Please open the door.'

Once again, Papa's words were like molten lava in Aniruddh's ears. His irritation was turning into anger. He had not been able to understand his father's behaviour to this day even though he was older now and his thoughts had begun to take shape. He would always ask himself why his father submitted to his mother. And in the absence of an answer he would suppress his resentment.

Like every other day, Papa had entered their room pretending nothing had happened. Akanksha and Aniruddh were used to this. Ever since they could remember, they had seen Ma either sulking or screaming. They would often cower in a corner when she lost control and both brother and sister would even cry together. But they had never mentioned their trauma to anyone outside their home and had not tried to ask for support from others. Even today, they had turned to their study tables quietly—Aniruddh in anger and Akanksha looking at her father with caring eyes. Akanksha's eyes would often well up and Aniruddh would feel a surge of love for his sister.

Papa had just begun walking towards the bathroom to wash his face when he had called out, 'Akanksha, dear, I'm feeling sick and my chest feels as if it's being squeezed...'

He gasped, unable to say anything beyond that. Both of them had seen their father fall to the ground. Before they could run to him, he had fainted. He was breathing but beads of sweat glistened on his forehead.

Recalling his father's plight, Aniruddh's eyes were filled with tears. Now he was feeling a sudden overwhelming love for his father. Heaven knows what state he was in in the hospital. He started knocking at the door of his mother's room again. Not getting any response, he went out into the garden and tried to peep into the room through the window that overlooked it. It was pitch dark inside the room and he could not see anything except the dark shape of the figure on the bed. The sound of heavy breathing told him that she was fast asleep. Still, he called out softly, 'Ma, wake up. Open the door. Papa is unwell. He has been taken to the hospital...Ma!'

There was no reply. Dejectedly, he walked inside slowly, towards the phone. Then he called the railway hospital to enquire about his father. Today, for the first time, he felt pity for his father, along with love.

The nurse from the hospital said, 'Your father is in the ICU. Doctors are examining him. There is no need to worry.'

Hearing this, Aniruddh sat on the chair outside Ma's room, defeated. What could he do? He could not even sleep, as worry about his father troubled him. How could anyone sleep in these circumstances? So his thoughts went back to those ugly scenes, only too familiar—ever since he could remember—when his mother would fight hysterically with his father. On several of those occasions he would switch the lights off and lie down on his bed, unmoving; on some days, he would listen to all of it silently, but at times when matters worsened, he would start crying. These days, he would not cry but the situation did disturb him.

But today, it was different. Papa was in the hospital and Ma was lying like a dead person in her room. He wanted to tell her what Papa's condition was as soon as possible and he was full of fear that the worst could happen. His anger soon turned into self-pity. What a life! All his friends lived peaceful, contented lives. He couldn't share his sadness with them; on the contrary, he had to invent happy stories to narrate to them. But at times the situation at home would be so chaotic that they had to go without food for days. Why was this happening to him? What had he done to deserve this? Immersed in these thoughts, he found himself crying, just as he did when he was younger. All his grief seemed to pour out in a heavy torrent.

3

AMIT was lying motionless on the hospital bed. He had still not regained consciousness, but the enzyme injection and oxygen had helped his heart work better and he was stable now. Seeing this, Aditi told Akanksha to rest in the next room but she stayed with her father. Amit's hands in hers, Aditi was sitting next to him on a stool, waiting for Dr Khurana. She would often glance at the ECG graph, disturbed to see Amit—her childhood friend—in this state. She wanted to hug him tightly and could not stop herself from stroking his forehead. She was feeling angry with herself. Amit had often tried to share his pain with her but she had always misunderstood that need for support as love and attraction. She was beginning to understand Amit's pain today. She had known Nikita for a long time and her behaviour was not new to her but Aditi had not expected the situation to be this bad. She kept looking at the clock and then at Amit's face. Her only wish at this stage was to see her friend on his feet again. She was praying for the night to end somehow and for Amit to regain consciousness. For the first time, she actually asked God for something. Her relationship with the Almighty was not too strong, but today she prayed, not for herself, but for someone else, someone dear to her. She wished she had listened to all that Amit had to say in the past and now vowed that she would give Amit the love and care of a good friend even without his asking for it. This feeling became so strong that she got up and kissed his forehead gently and said, 'Amit, nothing will happen to you. You will be absolutely fine.'

She didn't even realize when her eyes had filled with tears. Akanksha was watching her as she stood at a distance. She had heard that Aditi Aunty was a childhood friend of her father's but she had not imagined the bond to be this strong. Suddenly, the nurse's voice broke Aditi's reverie.

'Madam, there is an emergency case.'

'What happened?'

'The patient is in a serious condition. He has diarrhoea and is bleeding too. His body has lost so much liquid that he has fainted.'

'How old is he?'

'He must be somewhere between thirty-five to forty, madam.'

'Anyone with him?'

'His wife. She is crying piteously. It seems he drinks a lot. He is Dr Amit's patient.'

'Do we have an empty bed?'

'Yes.'

'Admit him and give him intravenous glucose.'

'Yes, madam.'

'I will be there.'

She wiped her eyes before her tears were seen by others, smoothened her hair and after appointing another nurse to stay with Akanksha and Amit, headed towards the patient. As soon as she reached him, she scolded the patient's wife without even asking her any questions. When the woman's crying didn't cease, she realized that she had vented the anger directed at Nikita on that poor woman. The woman pleaded with Aditi to save her husband's life, saying that she was like God for her. Aditi made herself calm down and turned to the nurse.

She asked, 'Where are the case papers, Sister?'

When the nurse gave her the patient's hospital file, Aditi examined the case papers and found that the patient had suffered from ulcerative colitis, for which a colonoscopy had been done earlier, revealing ulcers in the large intestine. He had then been given the sulphur mesacole treatment.

'Has he not been taking his medicines?' Aditi asked the woman.

'He has...we were unable to get medicines from the hospital in between...' the woman said with lowered eyes and then, with the corner of her pallu in her mouth, 'at times it is difficult to get medicines from the market, Doctor Sahib.' The woman folded her hands in front of Aditi in supplication.

'He has to take those medicines all his life. Don't discontinue them.'

She knew how it would be financially difficult for the family of the patient to do what she was saying. Was it possible for a household that barely manages two meals a day to buy those expensive medicines? Moreover, not only were medicines not readily available in government hospitals, it was likely that they were contaminated.

Aditi asked the woman, 'A test had been done by inserting a tube into the large intestine. Do you have its report?' The woman nodded.

'Bring it tomorrow. Don't give him anything fried or spicy. And no alcohol.'

'He seldom drinks these days,' the woman said in his defence.

'He won't die if he doesn't drink. But will die sooner if he does, understand?'

The woman touched Aditi's feet humbly. Aditi said in a softer tone, 'It's all right, don't worry. He will be fine.' Then she told the nurse, 'Steroids are necessary, start that. Show me the colonoscopy report tomorrow when she brings it.'

When she checked the patient's BP, she found it to be very low and told the man's wife, 'Give him porridge, absolutely plain. No milk or tea. You can give him curd. I hope he doesn't have fish and meat. Stop all that, you understand?'

Aditi knew that if a doctor began worrying about what the patient's family could afford or not, it would become impossible to work. Her job was to tell them what to do, clearly and concisely. The patient's wife nodded as if she understood every word, but Aditi put all the instructions down in the case paper and rushed back to the ICU.

The light was on in the room. Akanksha and the nurse were

standing on one side and Dr Khurana was examining Amit. 'What happened, Aditi?' he asked on seeing her.

'It looks like acute MI, sir. He vomited, there was frothing at the mouth and he was sweating. His breathing was blocked. He is not fully conscious and the blood pressure is very low.'

'What have you administered to him?'

'Nitroglycerin, morphine, enzyme and oral aspirin.'

'Show me the ECG.'

Dr Khurana looked at the old ECG report while checking the ECG monitor and then suddenly asked Akanksha, 'How are you, dear?'

Akanksha was teary-eyed. She could not utter a word. Dr Khurana stroked her head lovingly and said, 'There is no need to worry. Everything is under control because of the timely treatment. Be brave, beta. Is your mother all right?'

'Yes,' Akanksha said hesitantly.

Dr Khurana spoke to Aditi for a while, asking her to get a blood test done and then told the nurse to check his blood pressure. He asked Aditi to see him with the test report in the morning and left after putting everything down on the observation admit card.

The nurse whispered into Aditi's ear, 'Madam, there have been several calls from your family.'

'Tell them I am fine and will be back only in the morning,' she replied to the nurse.

Then she turned to Akanksha, 'Beta, go to sleep. Papa is fine now.'

'No, Aunty, I will stay with Papa.'

On hearing this, Aditi stroked Akanksha's cheeks with affection.

Just then the nurse from the maternity ward came and said softly, 'Madam, a delivery case needs attention.'

'Who is it?'

'Mrs Srivastatva, the wife of the signal inspector.'

'Where is she?'

'In the labour room.'

'Is she ready? Is the labour pain...'

'No.'

'Give her a drip. I am coming.'

'Srivastavaji has been asking for you.'

'I said I am coming!'

'Okay, madam. How is Doctor Sahib doing?'

'He is under observation.'

Aditi sent the nurse away and holding Akanksha's hands in hers said, 'Nothing will happen to your father. He is a brave man. I have known him since childhood and he has always shown courage.'

'But why do terrible things happen to Papa so often?'

Aditi was surprised to hear this. Akanksha was right, she thought, Amit's childhood had not been an easy one. She exhaled deeply and tried to soothe Akanksha again, 'Lie down here, beta. You will get tired. Rest for a bit. We are here to look after him.'

'And what about you, Aunty?'

'I will have to go for that delivery, beta. Don't worry, Sister is here.'

Akanksha asked wearily, 'Don't you get tired, Aunty?'

'I do, but I am used to it by now. A doctor's life means being on constant alert, beta. There is no fixed time for someone to be born or to fall sick, and then, everyone wants the doctor to look after each of them personally. It is not possible and is not even necessary. But we do give our time to patients as much as possible. Your father, for example, worries about each of his patients. He is very popular and everyone wants to be treated by him because he is famous as a good doctor. You might not know this about your father.'

As Aditi walked towards the labour room, what she knew of Amit's life flashed through her mind. She reached the labour room and examined Mrs Srivastava. There was still time for the delivery.

She said with mock anger, 'I had told you to do some physical work. But you people don't exert yourselves physically and that is why childbirth is so painful for you.'

'I did, doctor.'

'What did you do? Nothing? You should have mopped the rooms, swept them...all this is important. There is nothing to feel ashamed of. It seems Mr Srivastava didn't let you work. He must have called in an army of helpers. Isn't that so, Mrs Srivastava?'

Mrs Srivastava was trying to smile. Her husband seemed to be in more pain than she was. He had trailed behind the doctor and would have entered the room if he wasn't aware of Dr Aditi's temper.

'Doctor, I hope there is nothing to worry about,' he asked as soon as Aditi came out.

'Why do you people worry for no reason? Please wait for some time. It is always better if things are allowed to happen naturally. It is easier to operate in that case. They would have cut open the stomach within minutes if this was a private hospital and it would have cost more, too. Please wait, everything will be fine. I will be here, in the hospital.'

Mr Srivastava stood silently with folded hands. Like most relatives of patients in Aditi's care, he was abject and grateful.

Aditi returned to the ICU after instructing the nurse. Akanksha was drowsy but she had refused to lie down. She did not want her father out of her sight even for a minute.

Aditi sat down for a moment and looked at Amit. Again, some memories of Amit's childhood flitted across her mind. She thought, 'Perhaps I'll remember an incident, a funny one, that I could narrate to Akanksha to cheer her up.'

4

AMIT was semi-conscious now. His hands felt warm and he was a little surprised to find himself in the hospital. The lights were out so it was darkness that he faced when he opened his eyes, but he could feel the oxygen tubes. The light filtering in from the verandah was piercing the darkness inside. He glanced sideways and saw Aditi sitting on the sofa in front of the bed, leaning her head on the backrest. Akanksha was lying curled up on the same sofa with her head on Aditi's lap. Aditi's hand was on her forehead and he could see that her hands stroked Akanksha's forehead from time to time. He was relieved. He could not make out what time it was, but then he saw the lit up face of the clock which showed it was 4 a.m. Being a doctor, he understood that he had been saved this time, but what about the next...? He became restless as this thought crossed his mind and the events of last night slowly came back to him. He was supposed to go to the hospital for night duty. He remembered the severe pain in his chest. He was going to freshen up and serve food to the children when he had felt the piercing pain in his chest which had progressed to his arms. The same pain had reached his neck and back too. The feeling of nausea had followed and he understood from his experience that he was in the throes of a major heart attack. The sweating and difficulty in breathing had told him that the attack was intense. Before he could say anything to the children, his eyes had closed. All of a sudden, he remembered how angry Nikita had been last night. She had forced him out of the room and had shut the door, sending him into spasms of anxiety, worrying about how many sleeping pills she could have downed.

He knew he was helpless in the hospital. Nikita had done this before and had come out of it somewhat unscathed and this was the only thought that gave him some relief. He was so broken, both mentally and physically, that he could not think straight. He did not want to live any more but was bound by his love for his children. He had been quite worried about Akanksha in the past few days, thinking of how he would stop her from going into the darkness. Somewhere, deep down, there was love and a sense of responsibility towards Nikita too. What would Nikita do if something happened to him?

It was strange for him to hear his own heart's vibration on the ECG monitor. He had saved the lives of so many people and had seen so many others being swallowed by death in this same hospital. Life and death were everyday matters for him. But it was different when he himself was going through it. He was neither happy about a life saved nor upset about a life lost this time.

He found a little comfort in knowing that he was a sincere, dedicated doctor who tried his best, in every case, to save his patient's life. Otherwise, except for his children, his life seemed meaningless, making him unafraid of death. He had reached a strange stage where both life and death had no meaning for him. While going through these emotions, he glanced at Aditi. He was aware of her sadness, too, but Aditi had never talked about her problems to him.

For the last few days, he had tried to keep distant from Aditi. Earlier, he would assert his possessiveness, but she had warned him that she would not take any of that. Her words had hurt Amit and to this day, he could not understand what had made him behave so aggressively that night when Aditi had warded him off. But Aditi had done the right thing. He was ashamed of his behaviour and Aditi, too, had avoided him somewhat, since that night. Earlier, he had tried to share his sadness with Aditi but she had not really encouraged him to talk. She never took him seriously. On the contrary, her rude behaviour had often hurt him. He wasn't one to talk to others much, but even today, he wanted to share his feelings with her.

He heard the door open and saw the nurse walk in. He shut his eyes but his mind was alert. The nurse recorded the ECG monitoring and checked his blood pressure. She noted everything down on the bed ticket, reported to Aditi and left. Through half-shut eyes, Amit saw that Akanksha was looking at him and he closed them once again. Aditi and Akanksha began whispering and the words reaching him worked like balm on his sore wounds because they showed deep concern for him. Aditi's words had always made him aware of the practical aspects of life and even now, she was consoling his daughter—telling her about life—explaining some things and hiding others.

Although he could not see Aditi's face clearly in the dark, his mind's eye could picture her oval, dusky face with those large, gleaming eyes, and the black bindi that added to its beauty. Was this the same Aditi he'd known since childhood? She was a smart, grown-up woman now and he, such a weakling!

Carried away by his thoughts, he had travelled back into his past. Looking back, it seemed that someone had designed him to live in vain. Perhaps it was because he had been at the doors of death, but he felt a strange detachment, a resigned acceptance of his fate, which had not allowed him much peace or happiness. Even when he did get a few happy moments, they were invariably followed by a sea of worries. He couldn't believe that he had survived so many hardships. He wondered how he had managed to get this far. He had not even reached the age of forty—then why did it seem like he had lived too long? What, when, how and from where had it all started? He didn't even know. He had had no control over anything. He had just continued living, almost like a dead man.

As he was reminiscing, he realized that the sadness in his heart was growing. When the pain in the heart can't find an outlet, it flows out of the eyes as tears. Lying on the hospital bed, he couldn't stop the tears rolling down from the corner of his eyes. Trying to put together the pieces of his life, his thoughts reached the place where his life had begun. That space was full of sadness and visualizing it pained him. But why hadn't he felt that pain earlier? On the contrary, he had faced all his problems as a child and had moved ahead. How? Possibly because there were a lot of caring hands that were present to guide him through those troubles then. But today, it was not so. His childhood had felt complete even with all the problems but now, his life seemed empty. He was somehow proud of the way he had faced his problems as a child. He closed his eyes and saw the locality where he had grown up, the same one he had not seen in years even when it was in the same city and suddenly, all the memories became vivid. Darjani mohalla, Ghamapur...and...Ma, Babuji, Supriya...

Section 2

5

AMIT was about nine years old then. He was an intelligent child and understood his sister's problems. He was aware of the limitations of Supriya's body and used to them since childhood. At times he would even help Didi in her little problems. Every individual's nature is different, changing and adapting itself according to the situations and stages of life. Whereas Amit was quiet and compromising even as a child, Supriya was irritable, dependent as she was on others for everything. But her irritation was harmless and it did not really bother others. She was an integral part of the family, and looking after her on almost a twenty-four-hour basis was accepted wholeheartedly by them.

Amit's father was a teacher in the primary school, but was happy and satisfied in his little world. Malti, his wife, had limited her world to Supriya and Amit, so much so that she couldn't spend too much time even with her husband. Cooking for her children was her sole joy and taking care of Supriya had become a part of her daily routine. Supriya was the darling of the Darjani mohalla, a lower-middle-class locality.

Sprawling within the old city of Jabalpur in the state of Madhya Pradesh was the crowded and bustling area of Ghamapur. This is where Darjani mohalla was situated, consisting of twelve houses—the number of houses giving it its name—'darjani' meaning a dozen. Due to continuous construction and repair work, the height of the Jabalpur–Katni national highway kept increasing, but the situation of this locality, barely fifty metres away from it on the right, hardly saw any change. On the contrary, it started getting waterlogged during the rains. The path that led to it had also become very narrow because of the shops that had come up on both sides. All twelve houses had roofs made of mud tiles attached to each other. Two adjacent houses shared a wall. The houses were so close to each other that anything even spoken softly and cautiously in one house quickly became common knowledge for the entire locality the next day. This mohalla was like any other in the country. People from various regions of the country stayed here, their way of life, behaviour, food habits and language different from each other. The only feature in common was the fact they were all lower-middle-class households. Mostly, they were fourth-grade employees working in the railways or in ordnance factories, their occupation handed down through a generation or two. All the families had been staying here for several years.

The first house on the corner was Sunita's. Her husband was a driver serving a seth, a rich businessman. Since her husband had died in a road accident, the entire responsibility of the household had fallen on Sunita's shoulders. She was an attractive woman and the seth, who saw her one day, was lured by her charms. He was unhappy with his own wife, but got such solace from Sunita that he visited her regularly. Sunita earned a bad name because of this but she didn't care. She openly accepted and declared her relationship, saying that at least she was associated with only one man. She was upfront and outspoken. Unashamed of her relationship with the seth, she argued that society was hypocritical in condemning a man–woman bond merely because it was not recognized as a legal marriage. Even when the seth's wife insulted Sunita several times, it had not affected her nor did she respond to her jibes. Her doors remained open for the seth, but if any other man as much as looked at her, she behaved as if she would scratch his eyes out.

Sunita's neighbour was Kamla Gupta. About forty-five years old, she was sharp and cunning, more so in comparison to Mr Gupta, her husband, who was a simpleton. Even at her age, Mrs Gupta was extremely fond of make-up and clothes and dolling herself up. Both her sons were grown up and her daughter had been married off, but Mrs Gupta seemed to be getting younger by the day and her desires seemed to be getting stronger.

If on one side of Malti's house was Kamla Gupta, the other side was occupied by Gita—a sweet, simple lady, but her husband, Mr Shukla was absolutely young at heart. Even after being a father of five, there was no gravity in his behaviour. Gita and Malti were the best of friends. They were quite alike in their views about life and the world, their likes and dislikes. On the other side of Gita's house lived Alka, with her old mother. She had educated and married off three younger siblings, shouldering the responsibility of making them self-sufficient. But by then she was past the marriageable age and resigned herself to looking after her old mother. Although her siblings respected her a lot and visited often, Alka knew that she had to spend the rest of her life alone. She had a reason to live till her mother was alive but she did not know what she would do after that.

Two South Indian families occupied the houses next in the row, one from Tamil Nadu and the other from Kerala—but both families were known as 'Madrasis'. The other houses in the row belonged to the Khatik family, and then the Sainis. The Saini's daughter-in-law, Usha, was also a good friend of Malti's. Malti, Usha and Gita often met for a chat. Kamla, though much older, would join in too and try to assert her superiority. After the Sainis's house were those of the Sonkars, the Patels and the Bengali family. When the Durga Puja festivities began, the Bengali family celebrated with great verve and it was their idol that the people of Jabalpur thronged to see during the puja.

All twelve houses were similarly constructed. A small verandah at the front, followed by a big room, behind which was another small room used as a kitchen. Behind the kitchen was a courtyard and in one of its corners was the bathroom. Now all the families had latrines, but earlier, they all used to go to the big naala, a dry drain, to relieve themselves—the women in the dim light of early dawn and the men in broad daylight. Until Amit began going to college, the locality had only one municipality tap with water available for only one hour in the morning and even less than an hour in the evening. But the families coordinated with each other to ensure that every household got enough water for themselves.

All the families lived in harmony but at times tempers would explode over some trivial issue and their fights would spill over into the streets as well. However, if anyone interfered with them or threatened them, all twelve families stood together, facing all odds as one front. All of them were different from each other in every way, but there was a strange bond that tied them together. Their fights too spoke of their mutual relations—in grief and in happiness, even in their fights, they were one.

6

JABALPUR is one of the oldest cities of central India. Situated on the banks of the Narmada, it is famous for Bhedaghat, where white marble rocks rise majestically from the Narmada banks. Stationed here have been several centres of army signals units since the times of the British; it also boasts of the national training centre of the department of telecommunications, a telecom factory, the centre of the department of quality control and a vehicle factory that makes trucks named 'Shaktiman' for the army. It is also said that a reserve of explosives lies hidden by the army somewhere in the hilly areas near Jabalpur and there is also the gun carriage factory and ordnance factory. With its crowded shopping hubs and masses of people, it can be said to be a metropolitan city.

Jabalpur is also known by its other name, 'Sanskardhani', since traditional sanskaras are observed in this city. People from all regions of the country have been coming here over the years as members of numerous national organizations set up here; or as workers in manufacturing units; or in connection with army jobs. Thus, all festivals—Diwali, Dussehra, Moharram, Holi, Raksha Bandhan, Christmas—are celebrated with great enthusiasm and fervour.

Jabalpur is famous for its Durga Puja. Hundreds of Durga idols and a nine-day grand festival brings all of Jabalpur—the rich and the poor—onto the streets of the city. Crowds spend several nights roaming the streets night after night on foot, making it impossible to ride even a bicycle on the streets. Every lane, every street and every intersection of the city boasts of beautiful idols of the goddess housed in elaborate mandapas. Every locality has an organizing committee which publicizes the year in which the mandapa was set up to show off how old they were. Artwork on the mandapas highlight pertinent social issues or display thematic pictures to popularize and uphold traditional Hindu values. When Amit was a child, and even now, there would be Ramlila performances at several places and it seemed like night never fell in Jabalpur in those nine days. Several Durga Puja committees are decades old and have even got concrete stages that are used year after year for cultural programmes.

How could the Darjani mohalla fall behind the others? Here, too, Durga Puja was celebrated with great pomp and show. Whereas the Sonkars and Sainis took care of the external arrangements, the Bengali family would busy themselves with the puja and worship the goddess with fervour. These three families practically stayed in the mandapa for the nine days of the puja, cementing the feeling of togetherness.

Every child of the locality would participate in putting up lights in the streets leading down from the highway. Even a guest visiting one of the families would become a part of the celebrations and members of the locality who had left the city, tried to come back and participate in the Durga Puja every year. In the same way, the families in the mohalla celebrated other festivals like Holi and Diwali as one big family.

7

MALTI was not alone when Masterji, as Amit's father was known, passed away. Masterji used to be the teacher of the entire locality—all the children, whichever class they were studying in, would come to him for help in their studies and Masterji would always be ready to address their problems. The entire neighbourhood had congregated in grief at Masterji's untimely death, giving Malti all their support. For thirteen days, all twelve families stayed together in such a way that it seemed they all had suffered a personal loss. Although Masterji's brother had come, he couldn't really find much to do, whether it was regarding arrangements for the funeral or other rites of mourning in the face of the love of the families of the neighbourhood. Malti had not had to worry about anything in those thirteen days. Yet, she had become very lonely, not being able to understand what had happened, how it had happened and what would happen in the future. Her mind was completely blank.

Masterji had been absolutely healthy and it didn't seem like he was suffering from any disease. However, the worry about his daughter was eating him up from inside. He never shared his pain with anyone, not even with his wife. It was not as if Malti would discuss Supriya's future with him, since couples in those times didn't really sit and discuss things. Amit was still young.

One night Masterji experienced a sudden pain in his chest. He used to sleep with Amit outside on the verandah while Malti slept inside with Supriya. He kept ignoring the pain thinking it was caused by gas. At around midnight, when the pain became unbearable and he started sweating, he woke Malti up. She, too, didn't quite understand what was wrong; she brought him a glass of water and started massaging his forehead. He kept looking at her for some time and Malti didn't even realize that he had closed his eyes forever because it seemed that he was still looking at her. She thought he had gone to sleep but the moment she lifted his arms to pull the sheet from beneath to cover him up, she realized that there was no life in them. She tried shaking his body as hard as she could but it was lifeless. And suddenly, she began screaming, 'Listen to me! Wake up!'

When there was no response, Malti screamed louder. Amit was a little boy then. He woke up hearing his mother's scream and started weeping when he saw how distraught his mother was. Malti pulled him close and called out, 'Supriya, come here! See what has happened to your father!'

Supriya, who didn't sleep much at night, started making strange noises while lying down. Malti ran out to call Gita. Once Gita was there, Shukla and Gupta woke up, and soon, everyone was in Malti's house. Shukla ran to fetch the doctor who lived nearby. The doctor arrived almost immediately, but when he felt Masterji's pulse, he shook his head slowly. It did not take him long to declare him dead. After that, Malti neither cried nor screamed; instead, her eyes became absolutely vacant. The women of the neighbourhood had started crying, their voices becoming more high-pitched. Supriya, then just a child, stared vacantly at the wall, while Amit sat close to his mother, clutching her saree. The women were saying that Malti should be made to cry, otherwise she would go mad.

One woman said, 'Now what will happen to her? What a calamity!'

Another was screaming loudly, 'Oh Masterji, where have you gone?'

Another lady was howling, 'Why did you leave these children behind?'

All the ladies who came to condole would, without a word, hold on to Malti and cry first. Some would express their grief and cry sitting in front of Malti. Others would come in sobbing from behind their pallus or would enter the house howling. Outside, the men were discussing what was to be done next. Shukla and Gupta were at the forefront as they were the nearest neighbours. Saini, who was the eldest amongst them, and the Bengali and Madrasi families issued the order that, 'lest the family members take offence, at least Masterji's younger brother should be asked to come.' But how would they get his address? Shuklaji's children asked Malti, but she had never thought about much, other than what was to be cooked, neither was she ever asked about things. Now, should she grieve for her dead husband, join the neigbours in crying or look for her brother-in-law's address! And over and above that, she had no idea about practicalities. The younger brother was a frequent visitor, thus, the people in the neighbourhood knew about him. Everyone tried to think of what to do and finally, one of the sons of Saini was dispatched to send off the telegram.

Amit sat down quietly when he was tired of crying.. The women from the neighbourhood took charge of the kitchen and the men began to prepare for the cremation. Once dawn broke, the elders started putting together items that would be needed for the cremation. Having finished all the work, they waited for the younger brother to arrive. On receiving no news from him till afternoon, they made arrangements to get the body taken to the nearby crematorium, where Amit performed the last rites. When they came back from there, it was already evening so all of them went to their houses to bathe. The women had been shuttling to and from their houses all the while.

Amit was still a child. Almost like a robot, he did whatever he was told to. However, he had understood that his Babuji was dead and the moment he realized that he was never going to come back again, he started crying. All the uncles from the neighbourhood were being very nice to him. At the crematorium, he could barely grasp the fact that his father had disappeared into the flames on the pyre. When he came back home, he cried, holding his mother's pallu and hugging Supriya, who was crying in her bed.

Within a few hours, Malti's life had changed completely, but she was still not very aware of the practical implications of this. Later at night, when her brother-in-law came, things started falling into place in the house. Malti did not quite fathom what the future held for her in those thirteen days as she got busy with work. The fact that rites and rituals make one forget one's loss is a great characteristic of the Hindu culture. In spite of all this, Malti took great care of Supriya. Anyway, what could Supriya do other than crying? She lay on her bed, weeping and listening to sermons of the pandit, who had been brought to the house to conduct the small after-death ceremonies. His words could not teach her much; they could not help her distinguish between good deeds and bad or between heaven and hell, but they told her this much that her father was never going to stroke her head again with love. Amit mostly sat next to her, listening to the pandit and holding on to a corner of his mother's saree. The thirteen-day period passed like this and then the big question faced the family: 'What would happen now?'

8

TIME does not stop for anyone. With a person's death, the lives of those related to them changes, but does not stop. Her brother-in-law had left after consoling her and from here began Malti's new life. The wheel of time was moving at a fast pace. Being a lower-middle-class family meant being a little above the poverty line. A few problems or debts and one could easily slip to or below the poverty line. The people who belong to this group have enough to eat and a roof on their heads, but they don't have anything like a bank balance or any expensive household items. If one tries to aim for much more than one's daily bread, it could lead to a lot of problems. Masterji and Malti both came from the same economic background and had a similar worldview. Thus, there was an unspoken agreement between them that they would be content with what they had. Neither of them had any big dreams and nor did they desire much. They just wanted to have a basic but delicious meal twice a day that was earned with respect and God had been kind to them in providing this.

Masterji and Malti believed in simple living. They ate good food but wore inexpensive clothes. Malti did not even know much about fashion and modern trends. She was naturally beautiful and would always be dressed in a simple sari that she would wrap around herself, carefully covering up her whole body. She would make simple dal roti for lunch and would add a curry or some vegetables to the dal roti for dinner. Masterji would have dinner by 8 p.m. and then go to sleep. There was no provision for any enterainment, not even the radio. He read the newspaper every day, and at times a magazine from the school library. His only interest was reading. He kept away from the internal politics of the school and didn't have too many friends. However, if there was anything important to be discussed, the teachers from the school would visit him at home, while he would visit others only on special occasions. His parents had passed away long ago and his brothers had moderately paying jobs. The house in Darjani had belonged to Masterji's ancestors and his salary was enough to pay for the other expenses of the family.

Some time back, Masterji had met a life insurance agent. He had never thought of investing earlier but had understood that the agent was pressing him so much because he must be getting some commission. However, after a lot of cajoling from the agent and following his friends' advice, Masterji said yes to a life insurance for five thousand rupees. It was possible for him to pay the premium for this amount.

A few days after the thirteenth day after Masterji's death, the life insurance agent had suddenly come to their place. Malti had opened the door for him. She stood there with folded hands and her white sari covering her head. Her eyes were vacant and face sad. The agent had visited them earlier when he was getting the insurance done. It was difficult for Malti but was a part of the daily duties of the agent. He took out some papers from the briefcase and asked her to sign them. Malti wrote her name on them sadly, absentmindedly, without asking him what the form was for.

The agent said, 'I am very sorry. I will try to get you the money as soon as possible. Masterji had got his life insured only some time back, so there can be some problems, but...'

She cried after closing the door behind him. Amit was at school but Supriya had wept with her.

Time was moving at its own pace but it seemed to move faster for Malti. It had been weeks since the agent's visit and they had still not received any money. If a person passes away soon after getting an insurance done, it is called an early claim and such cases are investigated by the insurance company as they want to ensure that the person was not lying or critically ill. Malti didn't know any of this. She suddenly thought of asking Saini for advice and went to meet Usha in the morning.

'Oh, Malti! How are you?' Usha asked.

'Nothing important…just that we are not getting the insurance money,' she replied softly.

Usha was a close friend of Malti's. She understood that Malti was in desperate need of money. This too is a strange part of life—one cannot grieve for the dead forever. Malti needed money to feed herself and the children, and in order to get that money, she would have to keep all her emotions at bay. She had to consider the insurance not of life, but of death, a bargain that was not the law of nature but that of society.

'You don't worry. I'll talk to him.' Usha spoke to her husband and Mr Saini ordered his son to go to the insurance office straightaway.

The younger Saini, too, was intelligent and could handle difficult situations. He could be assertive and even aggressive if the need arose. He reached the insurance office and got to know that Masterji's was an early claim case and that an officer had already gone around the locality twice to investigate the matter—nobody was ready to say that Masterji had not been sick before his final illness. Saini was surprised. Masterji didn't have any enemies who would do this, but he also understood that ignorance is the biggest enemy of mankind. Not knowing what the enquiry was for, people must have refrained from saying anything to the officer.

Saini went to the senior manager and said, 'You can take it from me in writing, Masterji was perfectly healthy. God knows how this happened so suddenly…maybe this was God's will…'

'But how can you say this with certainty?'

'I can because I have never seen him very unwell. I am his neighbour.'

'Can you get an affidavit from a doctor confirming this?'

Saini stopped for a second and then continued, 'Why not? I have never seen him unwell…but, if he had never been ill, how would he have known any doctors? And in that case, why and how would anyone write a guarantee for him? However, you can ask the people from the school he taught in...had he ever taken sick leaves?'

The manager saw reason in Saini's statement and asked his officer to get a certificate from the school authorities. Saini returned and told Malti that the matter was on the way to being resolved.

Malti had begun to understand the ways of the world. The certificate had been issued and she would get the insurance money soon. She really needed the money then as she was hard-pressed for even two meals a day. The debts were piling up. She would go to Saini's place every day to ask about the claim and Saini, too, had started visiting the Life Insurance Corporation office daily at Usha's insistence.

And finally, Malti got the money. She had heaved a sigh of relief on getting it—the cost of her husband's life had become her support for subsistence. However, she did not see these intricacies of emotions in this paradox. Knowing that money would not now come easily, she had reduced the amount of milk she bought from Lalan, the milkman, to almost a half of the earlier amount—now only enough for two cups of tea for each morning and evening.

9

THE upper, middle and lower classes—these are the three categories society can be divided into, but there is a huge gap between the upper class, which has status, money and property in abundance and the lower class, which has a shortage of everything. But the middle class that falls in between can be divided into three categories: the upper middle class that aspires to join the ranks of the 'upper class'and hates being called 'middle class'; the middle middle class is one that is just that—in the middle; and then there is the lower middle class which exists on the border between middle and lower. A slight mistake and they can slip into the lower category.

Masterji was a teacher in a privately owned primary school in Jabalpur. On the face of it, a teacher is one who leads from the front and works for the better future of society by showing the right path to the next generation; but in the great country of India, the plight of primary school teachers is deplorable. They are no better than daily wage labourers. They barely earn enough to feed their children and the fact is that a lot of schools have come up to meet the demands of the growing population but they are not administered well. The management of these schools might be earning some money but both the teachers and students are left empty-handed.

Malti and Masterji had not asked for much in their lives. Their desires and needs were very limited and they were satisfied and happy with what they had. It was in their nature to be happy. Happiness is a state of mind; it does not come from possessions.

Amit remembered how he would go to the Gurandi market to get vegetables with his father on his bicycle. They would buy fresh, green vegetables after a lot of bargaining and at times would get cheap seasonal fruits. Even one mango was enough to fill the entire season with a happy fragrance...and now, even if he had a mango every day, he never got the same happiness from it. Amit used to accompany his father to get coal and wood for cooking, instead of kerosene, which was expensive. The chulha, stove, was used only for making tea. Every morning and evening, food was prepared on the chulha—the taste of the food cooked on the coal fire had a deliciousness of its own. Happiness and satisfaction was hidden in the small pleasures of life in those times, and he never again got the same satisfaction as that of eating simple food with his family, sitting on the floor, on a Sunday afternoon. Supriya would also eat with them, lying on the floor.

The entire neighbourhood was made of lower-middle-class families but the situation of those who had fourth grade government jobs was better than the rest. And if there were two earning members in the family, they were even better off. Some of them had even bought a moped and some households had record players. Malti would go to the Sainis's house to listen to some old songs on their music set.

Amit used to get the required nutrition from the simple chapatti and vegetables cooked at home. Life was good till Masterji's untimely death. It had been several months since Masterji passed away and Malti now stood at the threshold of the lower middle class. There was no other source of income and there were no savings. How long would the life insurance money last?

Lalan was a kind man and insisted that Malti should continue getting her supply of milk from him. He said, 'Continue taking a quarter of a litre. At least there will be some milk for making tea. Give me the money later.'

The grocery shop owner, on the other hand, had started throwing tantrums because Malti could not pay her bills. Sunita had been through this herself and she could read the pain in Malti's eyes. One day, she offered some money to Malti. When Malti refused to accept the money, Sunita said, 'What do you think? That I am doing you a favour? Or is my money tainted? Look, I did not marry anyone else after my husband passed away, but I have been with only one other man. The world may call me a bad woman, but do you also believe that I have relationships with various men? Even I have to bring up my daughter; a driver's wife can't become a driver, neither can I work as a maid nor beg. One man has taken the responsibility of looking after me and I have been loyal to him. He takes care of my daughter, isn't that enough? I can understand your plight because I have gone through this and therefore I want to help you. Now take the money if you want to—I won't plead with you all day long.'

Malti gave her friend a wan smile but could not bring herself to take the money.

Malti was a simple-minded woman. She did not know what to do. The money that she had got from the insurance had been used for the expenses for the last four to five months to pay off the debts incurred during the death ceremonies. She had understood that her lack of education had become a curse now. It was very difficult for her to get a job at this stage of life, and without any contacts. Amit was too young to help.

10

ONE morning, that simple-minded, inexperienced woman stepped out of her house. She had never met Guruji but had seen him from afar and heard a lot about him from Masterji who had told her that he was a good Samaritan, a Brahmin not only by caste but also by his deeds... He was the principal of Masterji's school and was popularly known as Guruji. Since Malti could see no other way out of her predicament, she decided to go to him.

She had never stepped out of the mohalla alone as she had to be at home to look after Supriya who, necessarily, was the focus of Malti's life. She took Amit along but could not leave Supriya alone. She requested Gita, 'Please stay with Supriya for some time, I am going to the school to meet Guruji. I want to ask him to give me a job in the school.'

Supriya could not speak but communicated her thoughts to Amit and Malti through her expressions and that day her eyes seemed to say, 'I will be fine. Don't worry.'

Amit was young but aware of his responsibilities. He studied in the same school so he showed Malti the way. They were waiting outside Guruji's office patiently. Malti's mouth was going dry due to nervousness and her heartbeat quickened.

When Malti and Amit entered the principal's room, Guruji was surprised to see her. He stood up and said affectionately, 'Beti! How are you? You should have called me...I would have come to your place.' Then he requested them to sit down.

Covering her head with her pallu, Malti sat down. The sadness in her eyes spoke volumes. She just managed to say, 'Guruji, now only you can guide me and tell me what to do next.'

Guruji looked perplexed. One understands the worries of

others, at times even empathizes with them, but unless one suffers the same pain one cannot know the intensity of it—and a clear solution rarely presents itself in all clarity. However, Malti had spoken with absolute simplicity and ease. There was no pretence, there was no dramatic show of emotions and sadness. It was her reality and she had accepted it as such. Her children had become her only reason to live. She knew this now. She had suddenly grown up into a mature woman and the innocence in her face had been replaced by a certain maturity.

Guruji could sense those changes in her. He was a simple, spiritual, hardworking man, and even though he did not know how to solve Malti's problem, he was not someone who could turn away and simply say that he could not do anything to help. After staying silent for a few minutes, he said, 'Tell me, beta, what do you want?'

Malti remained silent, unable to voice her request for a job. How did it matter what she wanted? It wasn't as if her wanting could change anything. Guruji understood.

'Okay beti, you go home. I will do something for you...' Guruji could not say anything beyond that. He didn't even know what he could do for her.

Malti bowed to him and slowly walked out of his office. There was no room for tears in her eyes any more. If there was no smile on her face, there was no agitation either. She had nothing to lose anymore.

She stopped at the grocery store to get some provisions for the house and the shopkeeper said meaningfully, 'Don't worry, sister. Give me the money when you have it.' Malti did not know what to say. She could have done nothing if he would have refused to give her those essential items. She picked up the groceries and came home.

Gita was sitting next to Supriya, talking to her. Supriya looked happy to see her mother and brother and Malti sat next to her without a word. She had tried to hide her sadness behind a fake smile but had failed.

Seeing his mother in despair, Amit said, 'Ma, don't worry... just wait till I grow up and become a doctor...I'll treat Didi and never let you suffer...'

Happiness lit up Supriya's eyes and a smile of surprise ran across Malti's face. She pulled Amit closer, hugging him, and stroked Supriya's head. Gita beamed at the little family, relieved to know that Amit had given his mother some hope. Then she said, 'I have to go home, but please call me whenever you need me.'

After sitting there for a while, lost in nothingness, Malti got up and said, 'Come, Amit, wash up and I will cook something for you to eat.' Malti cooked some dal-chawal and Amit, who was really hungry, quickly began eating.

'Beta, please feed your Didi too.'

Amit was feeding Supriya from his own plate and suddenly he said with a lot of love, 'Ma, why aren't you eating?'

Malti didn't feel like eating. Today, Amit's words had given her a new reason to live. A ray of hope. For the first time she felt that she too had some strength. If there was a problem facing her, there was also a solution to it. There was someone to share her worries, to hold her hand and help her. She felt that she had a future and for the first time, she too wanted to do something—not for herself, but for her Amit. She knew that even as a little boy, Amit not only loved Supriya but looked after her. Supriya would order him around. She liked to assert her right over him and even vented her anger at him. He would accept all her annoyance and irritation with calmness. This calmness was, in fact, becoming his natural behaviour. He did not feel any pity for Supriya—it was just his love for her, a bond that he treasured. He understood his responsibility towards her and considered it his duty to look after her.

'Ma, don't worry...just wait till I grow up and become a doctor...I'll treat Didi and never let you suffer for anything...' These words were ringing in Malti's ears. It seemed as if someone had sprinkled water on the hot dry earth of her future and tiny seedlings were beginning to sprout there. For the first time in her life, she was beginning to envision a future, she had found a destination she wanted to reach. She knew now that she had to live for her children, that she wanted to do something for them, and that there was life beyond cooking at home. And suddenly, tears started flowing from her eyes, mobilizing her self-confidence in a strange way. She again pulled Amit close. Supriya's body was handicapped but she understood everything and was overwhelmed to see Ma in this emotional state. She tried to move her hands to wipe off her tears but, like always, she could not do so, however hard she tried. Malti calmed her down, saying, 'Beti, don't worry, I am alive still and the three of us are going to be fine.'

Amit, who was half as tall as his mother, snuggled against her. He wished that he was older and felt for the first time that he should grow up quickly. He was not interested in living in dreams, how could he? Even dreams need some sort of a surface to stand upon, and he was struggling to come to terms with his now shaky life. He felt a determination, his self-belief, slowly strengthening his mind. He knew he had to fight, to assert himself. He wanted to eliminate the worry he often felt. His young mind understood that he was tied to two people whom he loved and he wanted to protect them too. He would change their situation some day, he felt. He did not know how he would do it, how would he change things. And his new-found self-belief grew even stronger as he vowed that he would take himself and his loved ones out of the dire straits they were in.

11

'COME fetch the milk, beti.' It was Lalan at the door.

Like he did every day, Amit called out to his mother, 'I'll get it, Ma,' and went out, carrying a small steel bowl.

Lalan asked, 'Where is your mother, beta?'

'She is with Didi.'

Amit looked at Lalan with his innocent face. He had seen Lalan bring milk to their house since he was a child and was fond of him. Lalan said, 'I will wait here. Please tell her to come and speak to me.'

Amit called his mother, who was sitting next to Supriya, 'Lalanji is asking for you.'

Malti covered her head with her pallu and went out, folding her hands in a namaste. Lalan hesitated a little and finally said, 'Sister, I understand your situation, but my cow doesn't. I have to feed her in order to milk her...and for that, I need money to buy her fodder. There is no hurry, beti, but if you could pay me a small portion of the amount, I could make do with that.'

This was not unexpected but was sudden. She lowered her eyes and said, 'I'll do something about it.'

'There is no hurry. Don't misunderstand me, sister. This cow of mine, she eats a lot, and does not understand. You don't worry,' he said, then hopped onto his cycle and sped away.

Malti didn't know what to do. How would she pay Lalan?

Just then, Sunita came out of her house, all decked up in a beautiful sari. She took one look at Malti and asked, 'What happened, why do you look so worried?'

'Nothing's happened.'

'I had asked you to let me know if you needed money. It's up to you.'

If there was a certain spontaneity and concern in her words, there was also the ring of a complaint. All the women of the locality would chat with Sunita but were eager to stamp her as a 'bad woman' the moment she went away. And with that, they felt assured that they would never lose their sacredness as faithful Savitris. Sunita was well aware of their attitude, but she was sure of one thing. Malti would never badmouth Sunita.

As she went on her way, she said once more, 'Malti, think about it!'

Then Gita came to Malti's house and told her, 'You should ask Guptaji for help. I'm sure you are aware of what my husband is like, that is why I'm not suggesting that you ask him.'

Gita and Malti were very good friends. Whereas Gita was a simple woman who didn't talk much and had an adjusting nature like Malti, Gita's husband was a smart, cunning and lecherous man. He would not let go of a chance to flirt with a woman. Sunita had warned him several times and one day, when he gave her a suggestive leer, she grabbed his throat, letting go only after Gita pleaded with her. The same Shukla had tried to be very friendly with Malti, too, so she avoided him. On the other hand, Kamla Gupta was a smart woman with a caustic tongue and her husband was a sweet, good-natured man.

Malti now understood the world like she never had before. Earlier, Gita, Malti and Kamla would chit-chat every morning after the men had left for the day, with Kamla doing all the talking. Sunita, who stayed in the far corner of the mohalla, would always speak to them for a few minutes every day. All the families had a cordial relationship with each other, but these three were quite close to each other. It was owing to this closeness that Malti had summoned enough courage to asked Guptaji for help sometimes.

But one day, through the thin walls of their house, Malti could hear Kamla screaming and shouting at Guptaji for this, 'What is the matter? You seem to be visiting Malti quite frequently these days! I am warning you! Don't you dare go there again or I'll break your bones.' Guptaji did not say anything in response.

Malti was amazed. Is this how relationships change when a woman becomes a widow? Was this what that long association with that family had led to? Could a woman, who called herself a friend, talk about another with such disrespect? Malti had stopped talking to Guptaji after that incident.

Guruji would visit Malti from time to time to ask her how the family was. Malti was amazed when she heard Kamla making sharp comments implying that Guruji had ulterior motives behind his visits. She was very hurt but Gita consoled her, telling her to ignore Kamla. There was a strange affection in the words of Sunita, who had a bad reputation, whereas Kamla, who was supposed to be Malti's friend, had only bitter things to say.

Malti confided in Gita one day. 'Gita, what should I do? I have spent all the money I had and my debts are increasing,' she said hopelessly. Perhaps it was her meekness that most people did not trouble her. The grocer had not refused to give her things on credit although he was rude to her. She knew she had to accept behaviour like this because she had to raise her children and it was vital to get what she could from people.

Kamla overheard the conversation between Malti and Gita and came out of her house. She gave her opinion in her shrill voice, although no one had asked for it, 'I have mentioned this before, why don't you get married again? How will you bring your children up? Supriya needs special care and Amit is too young. Think about this...else...you know what happened with Sunita...'

Kamla's words were like molten lead for Malti, but it was not in her nature to react—she was neither capable of it nor in a position to do so.

It was not like she cried all the time but the grief was making her weaker with each passing day. There was no source of income and she needed to feed herself and her children. There was no support from an almost non-existent family—her parents-in-law were long dead and her brother-in-law was barely being able to manage his own family. Her own parents were dead, too, and her brother, completely controlled by his wife, had not stayed in touch with Malti even earlier. The fact that she was not educated was another curse; she was not suitable for any job. Guruji could not help even when he wanted to. Gita would give her some rice, atta and other things secretly as she knew that if her husband got to know, he would try to take advantage of the situation. She tried to help as much as she could and was very troubled after today's conversation.

'Why don't you speak to Alka? She works as a headmistress of a school. She has brought up two younger brothers and is now looking after her mother. She is a strong person, a woman, I am sure she will understand,' Gita had rushed to advise Malti as soon as this thought crossed her mind in the middle of the afternoon. Malti thought it was a good idea and thanked Gita.

12

ALKA lived with her elderly mother only a house away from Gita's. Malti had decided that she would go and visit Alka that evening itself, after she returned from work. On the one hand, she was worried about the situation she was in and on the other, Kamla's jibes had left her disturbed.

Malti had begun understanding money and its management now. Savings don't last for very long in the absence of a regular source of income. Even the coffers of kings run empty if there is no regular, organized inflow of funds. Whatever little Masterji had saved and more than half of the insurance money had been spent on rites and rituals after his death. She did not know how important these rituals were nor was she in a position to refrain from following them. She had managed to spend a few months after that using the remaining money but it would not last very long. Amit was only in the fourth standard and she had to support Supriya for her entire life.

She was wondering what she would tell Lalan if she failed to arrange for money to give him by the next morning. The food supplies at home were more or less finished. It seemed that even when she was very careful—giving a little to Amit and Supriya and at times not eating at all herself—they seemed to be getting depleted at a very fast rate.

Malti was waiting for the evening so that she could see Alka. She was very restless, her eyes would go the clock repeatedly. Alka would return by 4 p.m. and Amit would be home by then so she could leave Amit with Supriya. As soon as it was time, she left for Alka's place feeling that she would find the solution to all her problems today.

She knocked at the door and someone asked, 'Who is it?'

Malti hesitated a little, 'This is me...Malti.'

Alka opened the door immediately and welcomed her, 'Oh Malti! Come in, how are you?' She had not even changed after coming back from school.

'Ma, see who is here,' Alka said to her mother, making Malti sit next to her bed. The old lady seemed to understand Malti's pain and was looking at her with tears in her eyes.

'Will you have some tea?' Alka asked.

'No, no, please don't bother.'

'What bother? I was making a cup for myself and will make some more for you.'

'Okay, sure,' Malti replied.

She looked around. The house was neat, with only the bare necessities. After her eyes roamed across the walls, she looked at the old lady, seeing love, compassion and a desire to do something for her in her eyes, but also a helplessness. And each time Malti would look away, trying to avoid those eyes that had spoken so much without the help of any words.

Alka came in with three cups of tea and some biscuits in a tray.

'So tell me, how have you been?' Alka asked, giving the tea to her.

Malti lowered her eyes. There were no tears but the emptiness in them had said a lot to Alka, and Malti's tears were flowing from Alka's mother's eyes today.

Malti adjusted her pallu and the words tumbled out, 'Can I get some work in your school?' She had thought of a lot to say but had managed to say only this much.

Earlier, the conversations between Alka and Malti had been limited to a polite greeting. Alka was the most educated woman of the locality and she kept busy. The difference between Alka's and Malti's level of education had prevented much communication between them and it was this that had prevented Malti from speaking her heart out in front of Alka, who anyway talked very little.

'How much have you studied?' Alka asked, gauging the situation.

'I…very little, no one had ever imagined…' she said hesitantly, lowering her eyes and then looking at Alka's mother.

'No, beti, whether it is a boy or a girl, we should educate our children, no one can predict the future. Life is not easy. The fire burning in the stomach and that of society—both trouble a woman more,' the experienced voice said, expressing wisdom in a few words.

'I have come to you…' she trailed off again, failing to complete her sentence.

'Please have a biscuit. See, I will not be able to help you if you don't tell me everything clearly,' Alka explained very simply.

'Didi, I don't know what to do,' Malti expressed her weakness in these words, accepting Alka's superiority.

'Amit is very young. I had hopes from Guruji, the principal of Masterji's school, but even he is not being able to do much because I am not qualified. I don't even know what I can do to help myself.' Malti said in one breath. Even now, there was no hopelessness, but only innocence in her eyes. There was hesitation but a search for her destination as well.

Alka had understood, being a worldly-wise woman. Everything was clear to her now. She said, 'Malti, I don't want to give you any false consolation but I will definitely do something about this.'

These words, which offered no immediate succour, shattered Malti's hopes. She could not wait even for a few moments. She would have to face Lalan and the grocer tomorrow. They were not troubling her for money as yet but she could not face them any more. She could not control herself any longer, 'Didi…now we are…' and the tears broke all barriers and flowed from her eyes. Her tears came out even heavier than the day that Masterji had passed away—that day it was the grief of losing Masterji but today, finding a way to live was proving even more difficult. Alka got up and hugged her as Malti wept bitterly. She had surrendered her silence in front of Alka who was her last hope.

'See, I understand your problem...but I can't give you an instant solution. I will try to do something as soon as possible.'

Alka wiped Malti's tears off just like her mother would have. Malti controlled herself and ran out of the house. When she reached home, Sunita saw her and followed her into the house. Malti had tried to avoid Sunita's gaze but she was not one to ignore Malti's pain. She entered and on seeing Amit and Supriya, said, 'So, children, how are things?'

Sunita would always speak to the children teasingly whenever she crossed their house. The children too were very fond of their Sunita Aunty. They did not know what she did and who she was. She might have been branded as a 'bad woman' by the other women of the locality but she was a loving person for the children.

Sunita stroked Supriya's forehead lovingly and pinched Amit's cheeks saying, 'Why don't you grow up faster?' Then she took Malti by the hand, leading her into the kitchen. She pressed two hundred rupee notes in her hands and said, 'This is just money which can be used to feed oneself, nothing more. It doesn't matter how it has been earned, but you need it now. If you want, you can return it to me later but keep it now.'

The authority with which Sunita had placed those notes in her hands had stopped Malti from refusing. Sunita left after giving the money to her but Malti stayed standing there for a long time. She was not even in a position to say 'no' considering the situation she was in. The tears rolled down her face as she wished she could wash away all the bad names that the women called Sunita. She controlled herself and after sprinkling some water on her face, she went to the other room, trying to behave as if nothing had happened.

'Amit, how was school today?'

'It was good, Ma.'

'Put your heart into it, beta. You have to study well.'

'Ma, I have told you, I will become a doctor.'

Amit's answer was a balm for Malti's wounds. Her own hunger made her think of the children and she went to the grocer's to get some provisions.

Today, her legs seemed to have some strength, the money in her fist giving her some energy. The grocer's scowl appeared on his face, but before he could berate her, Malti placed the note in his palm and said, 'Please keep this for now. I will return the remaining money soon…can I get some essentials…?'

'Sure, when have I said no?'

The grocer's smile peeping from behind his white beard had explained a lot to Malti. She was facing life and its reality every day but had managed to hold on to her pride till now. She knew now that it is money that speaks. She came home and lit the fire to cook, but realized the dal they usually ate had finished and it was too expensive to buy. It was important to give the children something to eat, so she decided to make only rotis…only those many that were needed and with that…pickle…no, salt and onions would be cheaper. She made the rotis, mashed an onion and sprinkling some salt over it, served it to Amit. He was confused to see this initially, but was too hungry to care. Holding the roti in one hand, he gave a bite to Supriya with the other. The dry roti made her cough. Malti made her drink some water and Supriya was prepared by the time she gave her the next bite. Malti was feeding Supriya but was immersed in her thoughts. What would she do if Alka, who was her last resort, refused? She trusted Sunita more now, but for how long could she take her help, too? She shivered at the thought. Thinking deeply, Malti didn't even realize when she had fed even her share of the roti to Supriya. She sat there trying to dissolve her dark worries into the blackness of the night. Amit was sitting next to her, studying. He often tried to read aloud to her, but this time, he was silent.

She spent the whole night staring into nothingness, contemplating how difficult it was to live and how easy to die. She got up with the first call of the birds in the morning, bathed and then prayed before the image of Goddess Durga. She had woken Amit up early and got him ready for school and now sat waiting for the time when Alka would leave for her school. She would go and meet her again. She knew that these were troubled times for her but she was determined to fight—for the sake of her children. Malti ran to meet Alka the moment she stepped out of her home.

'Didi, please do something.'

She didn't understand that such arrangements could not be made in such a short while. Alka had been through the same pain and didn't want to give her any false hopes but the way Malti had run up to her early in the morning moved her deeply.

'Look, Malti, don't worry. I told you, I will do something.'

'I will do whatever you ask me to, but please, don't refuse.'

'Malti, I…'

'No, I don't want to hear anything else.'

Malti was now standing like an obstinate child, holding Alka's hand. She was talking with such frankness to a woman she had barely spoken to in the last fifteen to twenty years. Alka, who had raised all her brothers and sisters and had spent her life running the household, was not bothered by this new responsibility. She knew how harsh life could be and how difficult it was to survive. She kept her hand on Malti's shoulder and said, 'You don't worry…'

These words were like heavenly nectar in Malti's ears.

'I will let you know. By the way, you can do any kind of work, right?'

Malti did not hesitate to say 'yes'. This was the only way out. None of her friends, except Sunita, nor her relatives had been able to help her; instead, she could see hope in a woman who she was not related to in any way.

Alka said again, 'Be patient.' Malti joined her palms in a namaste and rearranging her pallu on her head, went inside the house. She sent Amit off to school and after helping Supriya dress, she went to give money to Lalan, who'd arrived with the milk.

'Aa, aa.'

Supriya's voice startled Malti and then she realized that not only had she forgotten to feed her daughter, but had not given her any water either. Supriya had been observing her mother's condition for the past few days; she was not capable of speaking, but she understood everything. Her eyes told Malti that she knew what she was going through and Malti gently stroked her forehead. Supriya couldn't provide any support; on the contrary, she was dependent on others for support. She placed her head on her mother's shoulders, a gesture meant to tell Malti, 'Ma, I am with you in these difficult times. May God give me the strength to lessen your pain…' Emotions can be expressed through the eyes and her eyes were very capable of that.

13

MALTI still covered herself with her saree in the same way, the pallu on her head was still intact; the only change was that now she crossed the road more swiftly. However, the situation within the house had worsened. They had reached the stage of penury. They could barely manage a meal and would spend days just having water. The children had learnt to suppress the pangs of hunger. Malti had to resort to getting one roti from Gita every other day and feed it to both the children. She had lost all her appetite, surviving on water that just about kept her throat moist or a cup of tea from Gita. The darkness under her eyes had spread itself across the face. She had told Lalan to stop supplying milk and had said, 'I will pay the amount I owe you if I live to do it.' That had brought tears to Lalan's eyes, but what could he do? He, too, had to survive. Sunita had helped a lot but there was a limit to what she could do. Begging or death—there was no other option. Others in the locality were engrossed in their own lives and worries and none of them were rich enough to spare money.

That day, Alka had snatched away her last hope. What could she do? Two ladies were already working as maids in the school and the management had said no for the third one. She had said that she would talk to people in the neighbouring schools but was not sure how long that could take.

Then Amit came back from school and told her that the teachers were asking him to submit the fees as the next day was the last day for the submission. The house was immersed in darkness as the electricity connection, too, had been cut off due to non-payment of dues.

Malti was heartbroken seing the plight of her children, but she still had some life and strength in her. She thought she should go and meet Guruji, to ask him to ensure that at least Amit could continue with his studies. This was the dream she was living for. She could live without food or water, but she would not be able to live without any hope or dreams. She left for the school. Earlier, she used to follow people while crossing the road but now she had begun doing that alone. She was still not very fluent while talking to other people but had learned to articulate whatever she had to say in a few sentences. She had already gone to beg Guruji but he said the same thing to her over and over again. 'Beta, I have spoken to the president and the secretary of the organization. They have assured me that they will do something but we can't be sure as of now.' Malti would listen to this each time with a bowed head but today, it was a different matter.

She said, 'Guruji, I haven't been able to submit Amit's fees. The teachers have asked him to pay the amount for all the three terms that is due.'

'Oh ho! These school teachers just don't use their brains. Even when they know and understand everything, they will observe rules blindly. You leave this to me, beta. I will take care of this. I can do this much, at least. I will propose this today itself. Amit's fees will be waived. And yes, apart from the fees, the institution will provide him with books and stationery from the next session. After all, he stands first in the class. He is a brilliant student. It won't be difficult.'

Hearing this, Malti's face regained some of its lost brightness. She folded her hands in a pranam.

'Oh, there is no need for this. This is my duty. This can happen to anyone, it is destiny. I will keep trying to get you a job somewhere, Actually, my child, these days it is very difficult to get jobs, and the situation in private schools is bad anyway. How do I explain it to you...'

Malti knew that the reality was by then.

'But, beta, remember this. You have to educate Amit. He is

a very smart child. I will make arrangements for his education in this school itself.'

'I will not let his education stop while I am alive,' she thought. She was leaving his room when Guruji said, 'Meet Amit's class teacher on your way out and tell him that you have spoken to me about his fees.'

Malti reached Amit's classroom after asking for directions.

Amit saw her and stood up happily, telling his teacher, 'Sir, my mother is here.' Amit's teacher repeated Guruji's words and said, 'Please don't worry, sister, your son is very intelligent.'

These words would always brighten up Malti's face and today it felt like greenery in a desolate desert. She took Amit back home with the teacher's permission. She was happy today; it was a huge relief.

While walking back, she told Amit again, 'Son, you have to study a lot and become a big man some day.' Her words were slow yet strong like her pace, full of determination to reach their destination soon. Amit replied, 'Yes, I will study hard, but a big man...who is a big man?'

Malti didn't know the answer to that but she touched Amit's forehead lovingly and took him to the Durga temple that was on their way—she had to thank the goddess. But her feet seemed to be giving up, it felt as though her breath would leave her body. When she raised her arms, they were shivering. She bowed and thanked the deity and then looked into the eyes of the idol. She didn't even know how to ask the gods for boons. She was hobbling now so she sat near the stairs. Amit was standing next to her. The rays of the sun felt too strong and were hurting her eyes. She felt that life would seep out of her body. Her head was spinning and she held it with both her hands. When she opened her eyes, darkness confronted her. Amit's face was blurred and she could not even see the idol inside the temple. She tried getting up, holding Amit's hand, but fell to the ground. She put the prasad that she had in her fist into her mouth—she had not eaten anything in days and the prasad in her parched throat made her cough badly. Amit ran into the temple and got her a glass of water. The water after the prasad had given Malti some energy but she still didn't have the strength to get up. She rubbed her eyes and saw that a man was distributing packets of food to people outside the temple. He gave one to her too and she was suddenly reminded of Supriya, 'Sir, please give me one more. My daughter is at home.'

She urged Amit with a new-found energy. 'Take it, son. It is prasad,'...and Amit had spread out both his palms to receive it.

14

MALTI reached home and fell unconscious on the bed. For a few seconds, Amit was very worried, but he woke her up after some time and fed her the prasad and the food from the packet, little by little. Tears continued to flow from Malti's eyes and she hugged Amit lovingly asking him to eat, too. Amit was growing up and his hunger never seemed to subside. He had already finished eating the food from his packet and he was now feeding both his mother and Supriya, whose face seemed to be shrivelling up because of hunger. Malti had fallen into a deep sleep after having the food and some water, but she was unable to get up. She had grown very weak and it was difficult for her to move about.

Temple...prasad... After all, it was clean food...and Amit had found a way out of the clutches of hunger for his family and himself...it was as if the goddess herself had shown him the way. Now he went to the temple every day on his way back from school and collected all the prasad he could pack into his school bag and then gave it to Ma and Supriya. In the evening, when the other children were out playing, he would go to the Hanuman temple in the High Court grounds and bring prasad from there. When Ma asked him, he said simply, 'I go the temple to pray and bring back the prasad that I get there.'

Malti did not stop him. Amit could see his mother's deteriorating condition and one day, he had spoken about it before Supriya. He would share everything with his sister. Supriya wasn't much older than him, but she was helpless as far as her body was concerned. She would listen to Amit silently and after that evening, she had even stopped making the 'Aa, aa' sound. She would be alone at home for long hours these days as Ma had to spend a lot of time looking for work. Earlier, whenever she needed water or needed to relieve herself, she just had to call out to her mother, but now she would have to wait for her. At times, unable to control it, she would wet the bed. Malti never complained while cleaning the soiled bed, but Supriya would be filled with self-loathing if that happened.

Worries were living a life of their own but before death could knock at their door, Guruji came home one day. He looked very happy and as soon as he came in, he said to Malti, 'Beta, today I will have some tea.'

Malti ran to Gita's place and got him a cup of tea. Sipping it, Guruji said, 'Beta, if you don't mind, I have got a job for you. Keeping Masterji's work and contribution in mind, the management has decided to keep you as a nursemaid in the school. The position is not very good but you will not face any problems...it is just some cleaning and taking care of the children. They are paying a reasonable salary...if you don't have any objection, should I say yes to them?'

Even before Guruji could say anything about the money, Malti said yes. Beggars can't be choosers. The blood had started to rush through her veins in happiness and the joy of life could be seen in her face. She had a very limited aspiration—to be able to get two meals every day for the children. And since she could see that goal in sight, her relief was immense. As for the nature of the work, she considered all work equal and she had nothing to hide from anyone—her condition was known to everyone.

Guruji was a bit hesitant about offering this job because he thought the job of a nursemaid beneath her, Masterji's wife. But Malti was willing to do any work to bring her children up. Her parametres for right and wrong were very simple—she would not do what Sunita did, though she didn't see any fault in Sunita's choice.

Guruji's help was a boon for Malti. She bent to touch his feet as he was leaving and said, 'I will come from tomorrow, with Amit.'

Guruji understood and a smile came to his lips as he lifted his hands to bless her.

Malti was preparing herself mentally for the job when it suddenly struck her that if she went out to work, Supriya would be left alone at home. Supriya had gauged her worry and after a long time, gathered the strength and uttered 'Aa aa', as if saying, 'Don't worry, Ma, I'll be fine.'

15

A new life, new paths—Malti had started going to school with Amit. She had to face a few problems in the beginning. Some teachers accepted her happily whereas others looked down on her. She didn't raise a hue and cry about it, neither did she expect anything from anyone. She did whatever work was given to her wholeheartedly and slowly, over time, she made her presence felt there. Initially, Amit loved to have Malti around but at times, other students who were jealous of him, would say things that hurt him deeply. These comments would make him burn from within, but he put this fire to good use by studying even harder.

His education and books were financed by the school and now they could manage two meals a day—that was all Malti wanted. Her only desire now was to educate Amit and make him a successful man. Amit participated and excelled in debates, cultural programmes and sports and Malti observed her son's development with great joy. Finally, life was moving on...step by step.

16

ADITI was three or four years old when her father passed away in a road accident. She was called Gudiya at that time. Sunita seemed to have lost all reason, remaining grief-stricken for days, but slowly she pulled heself out of the darkness, realizing she had her daughter to look after. She did not have any relatives, so the people in the mohalla had looked after them for some time. Then Sethji started visiting. He would give her money and also a lot of love to Gudiya. On one hand, he was unhappy with his marriage, and on the other, Sunita was beautiful and needy and soon a new relationship developed between the two. Sunita became aware of the responsibility of bringing up a daughter when she started growing up—but she had already dedicated herself to Sethji by then. She would get worried seeing her daughter grow up into a young woman—what would she think? Sethji could not formalize this relationship into a marriage and she could not leave him. Her daughter was the apple of her eye—her only hope. So one day, after discussing the matter with Sethji, she sent Gudiya off to a boarding school in a big city. There was no dearth of money and the people at school gave her a new name—that is how Gudiya became Aditi.

Sethji had provided Sunita with all the household amenities she needed—a gas stove, fridge, she had everything. He even offered to get her a new house but she had refused saying, 'I have always lived here and know a few people here. A new place will bring new difficulties with itself.' All day she did nothing but dress up, listen to music and sing songs. She would spend the entire day waiting for Sethji, who turned up whenever he felt like it, which was not every day. She did not have any complaints, the only problem was, how to spend the time? She had sent off her daughter to another city because of the fear that her bad reputation would affect the young girl, but she missed her and would spend a lot of time thinking about her. Aditi would come home during the holidays—summer vacations and Diwali—and was growing up, knowing and understanding the relationship her mother had with Sethji. Now that she had come to know of everything, Sunita didn't want her daughter to stay away from her and Aditi, who missed home, wanted to lessen the loneliness her mother felt. So, she returned to Jabalpur. Sethji got her admitted into the convent school there and Aditi went on to study well and top her class. Sunita wanted her daughter to study a lot and not turn out like her—she wanted Aditi to reach a respectable position in society. She had enough money and didn't shy away from spending it on her education.

Aditi was in the same grade as Amit but in a different school. He studied in a local school whereas she was in a convent, where all the rich children of Jabalpur came to study. Though Aditi would get all the money she asked for, her attention was always on studying hard because Sunita had instilled the desire for success in her heart. However, she had to face some discrimination because of her family situation and the other girls often jeered at her. Thus, she didn't have any friends in school and would spend all her time alone. She would listen to their jibes quietly at times, but she would often fight back. As a result, a strange bitterness pushed her to work even harder.

Aditi was very close to her mother. She didn't think that her mother was wrong for being in a relationship with the seth. He showered her with love and affection and provided for them, becoming a father figure for her. She would not hear anything against him.

The relationship between Amit and Aditi was a simple, natural one. There was no competition between them. There were more differences than similarities in their family situation, in that Aditi was financially better off, but their motivation, values and ambitions were the same. Amit was a shade better at studies than her but Aditi never saw him as a rival.

Aditi didn't mingle too much with the people of the locality but she was fond of most of them. Aditi used to visit Amit often to discuss studies and Malti didn't seem to mind their growing friendship. With her bittersweet experiences, Aditi acquired a smartness, verging on hot-headedness, whereas the stamp of poverty showed clearly in Amit's softer personality, although he became increasingly assertive. Time was flying past and its effects were visible, with both Aditi and Amit progressing towards adulthood.

Supriya was as dependent on others but was used to staying alone at home when Malti went out to work. Often, someone from the neighbourhood would come to assist her. Saini's daughter-in-law, Usha, and Gita would visit when they found time during the day but it was Sunita who was always available for Supriya and took great care of her. Supriya too loved her like her own mother. Amit, too, was very fond of Sunita and although he visited their place very rarely, both Aditi and Sunita would bring him delicious snacks and both families would sit together and chat for hours.

17

THE Madhya Pradesh State Board was conducting the class X examinations. Amit had worked very hard for it, knowing that his mother wanted him to become a 'big man'. Though, he did not really understand what becoming 'big' meant, he knew he wanted to become a doctor. He had stayed up nights to study and Supriya would stay up with him.

Now the exams were over and he was sitting at home, talking to Supriya. It was a hot, summer afternoon, with not even a desert cooler at home. Even the fan had to be used judiciously to avoid a fat electricity bill. Since today it was hotter than usual, he had taken off his vest and was scanning the books he had got from the library when he was startled by a knock on the door. He then heard someone call out, 'Amit bhai, someone has come to meet you.'

Amit came out and saw two men on a scooter.

'Are you Amit?'

Amit nodded slightly.

'We need to speak to you.'

He got a little worried hearing that, but asked, 'Tell me, in what context?'

'You have secured the first position in the Class X exams of the Madhya Pradesh Board. We have come to interview you.'

For a few minutes, Amit could not understand what had happened. He ran inside to put on a shirt and came out buttoning it up. He felt a little shy on hearing their question, 'Do you have a photograph of yourself?'

'No, I am sorry, I don't have a photograph.'

'It doesn't matter. Please put on better clothes and I will click a photograph here itself,' the other gentleman said.

Amit ran in, picking up his lungi. The only good pair of trousers that he had were part of his school uniform, so he slipped them on. He didn't really need to change the shirt, and couldn't, because this was the only one he had. He combed his hair and stood looking at himself in the mirror. Then, on his way out, he kissed Supriya on the forehead. She had been watching Amit change in a hurry and was still puzzled about what was happening.

'Didi,' he said, and she was even more surprised. He, who always called her Supriya was calling her Didi today, 'I have secured the first position in the class X exams in the entire state.'

Supriya didn't know much about it but had begun to understand a little, hearing Amit's conversations. She started shouting 'Aa aa' in happiness. People from the neighbourhood had gathered outside the house and Sunita and Aditi, too, had come outside on hearing all the commotion. Aditi asked, 'What happened?'

The press reporters told her, 'Amit has secured the first position in the High School Examinations in Madhya Pradesh. We have come to interview him.'

Aditi ran into Amit's house jumping in joy and met him on her way in. She punched him and said, 'Congratulations! Now I will ask Aunty for a lot of sweets!' Her happiness echoed in her innocent laughter.

Amit had still not been able to actually feel his happiness and Aditi's words suddenly reminded him of his mother, 'I will just meet Ma and come.' And he ran to the school in his chappals, tearing through the crowd. There were not many people in the school premises because of the holidays and Malti was cleaning the garden next to the school building. Amit ran to her and held her close from the back.

'What happened? Is everything okay?' she asked.

By now, the happiness could be seen on Amit's face and he said, 'Ma, Class X results are out!'

Malti said, 'So, you must have passed with good grades.' Because of the time she spent in the school, Malti now knew a lot about studies and examinations.

Amit began jumping with joy and said, 'Ma, not just passed, I have secured the first position! Not just in the school, but in the entire state of Madhya Pradesh! Reporters from the newspapers have come to our place to interview me. My name and photograph will be published in the papers tomorrow!' Amit was almost screaming now.

Malti dropped the broom from her hands on hearing this. She rearranged her sari's pallu and there were tears of happiness in her eyes. She had never seen Amit so happy. Wiping her tears, she said, 'Come, let's go to Guruji and take his blessings.' Today, there was a lively spring in her step and her slightly stooped back had straightened.

Before Malti could tell Guruji the news, Amit started talking, 'Sir, the results for the High School Examinations are out. And I have topped the ranks in the state,' he said and bent down to touch Guruji's feet. Guruji touched his forehead in blessing and said emotionally, 'Well done...son! Keep working like this and earn a good name for your mother. This is all the result of her hard work.'

Malti lowered her eyes on hearing this. Before Amit could thank him, Guruji called a clerk in and gave him a hundred-rupee note, instructing him to get some sweets and to gather all the teachers who were present in the school at that time. Slightly confused, the clerk asked, 'But what happened, sir?'

Guruji said, 'The gods are kind to this boy—he has surpassed all our expectations! He has brought fame to the school...this boy will grow up into a great man one day.' Hearing this, Amit was again confused about 'greatness' but the excited clerk was already rushing to the market to get sweets. All the teachers came to Guruji's room and suddenly, Amit was the centre of attention. After spending some time with them, Amit expressed the desire to go home as he wanted to be with his mother and Supriya for some time and the press reporters too were waiting. Taking their permission, Amit walked out holding his mother by the shoulders and all eyes were on him.

On reaching home he saw that Sunita was bringing tea for the reporters. There was an atmosphere of celebration in the neighbourhood—everyone had gathered, discussing Amit's success animatedly. Sunita was expressing her happiness in a loud voice, forgetting all about her daughter, Aditi's results. Even Aditi had forgotten all about it.

'I always knew that Amit will do something noteworthy.'

Another said, 'Now, my brother, Malti's difficult days will come to an end.'

And someone else said, 'Amit, brother, don't forget us when you become rich.'

Answering the reporter's question, 'Who do you give credit for your success?', Amit replied, quite simply, 'To my mother.'

'What are your plans for the future?' At this question, he said, 'I just have to study a lot.'

Then the reporter asked, 'What do you want to become?'

'A great man.'

'What do you mean by "great"? You want to earn a lot of money?'

The innocent Amit could not answer this question and said simply, 'No, no, nothing like that. I want to become a doctor.'

The reporters left after clicking Amit's photographs. This was a golden day in Amit's life, showing the first positive change—a place from where he could see a new destination.

Since Aditi's school was affiliated to the central board, the CBSE, her results were yet to be declared. She didn't quite understand why she was so happy for Amit. All the women had congregated inside the house—Gita, Kamla, Saini's daughter-in-law Usha, and the women and children from the Bengali and Sonkar households. However, Sunita was the one who was the happiest; her excitement and joy knew no bounds today.

Everyone said that Malti should get them sweets. Malti herself was quiet, not knowing how to react to this sudden happiness.

After some time, she said, 'Why not? I'll get them right away.'

Before she turned to go out, Sunita said, 'I will send someone.'

Gita, too, was very proud of Amit and was about to offer to get the sweets. But how could Kamla bear to know that anyone else could get ahead of her in this celebration? In an attempt to score over the others, she said, 'Who will go to get the sweets? Wait, I will arrange for them...'

'Listen,' she said addressing her husband, 'Go to the Shakti Bhandar and get some boondi laddoos.' Guptaji was a simple man and always tried to oblige his wife. He picked up his cycle and asked, 'How many should I get?'

'Get enough for everyone—quickly!'

'How nice, today Kamla is treating everyone,' said Sunita.

'Why not? He is like my son.'

The neighbour enjoyed seeing Kamla, who never offered even a cup of tea to anyone and was always uttering bitter words, offering sweets to everyone today.

Amit's life had changed in an instant. Amidst the conversation and celebration, a gentleman entered the neighbourhood, trying to elbow his way through the crowd to enter the locality. By now the Sonkars had installed speakers and were playing songs loudly. This was Jabalpur's tradition, an entertaining aspect of its social life—playing loud music to celebrate any happy occasion. Sonkar Bhai had installed two speakers so that the music would boom throughout the mohalla. No one seemed to mind the noise except for the stranger who was trying to find his way around the place.

'...Does Amitji stay here? Can I meet him?'

The children were slightly confused, 'Who is this Amitji?' Suddenly, it struck Sonkar's son, 'Oh! He is referring to our Amit!'

'Arre, when did our Amit become Amitji?'one of the boys said, smiling.

'There, the house where you see a crowd...that is where Amit stays.'

'Badde*, you take him there.'

Amit was enjoying himself, participating in the celebration and tapping his feet to the music. The newcomer was introduced to him but he could not hear him over the din. The guest was carrying a garland of flowers and sweets in his hands. When he gave the sweets to Amit after shaking his hands, Malti intervened, 'It is we who should be offering sweets.'

The exposure to the world had taught Malti how to speak to strangers but she still had a lot to learn—it had not occurred to her to ask the stranger who he was even then.

After a while, the stranger himself spoke to Amit in a low voice, 'I am the manager of a coaching institute. First of all, I would like to congratulate you on your success.'

Amit was still a child so he was finding it difficult to assimilate all this happiness at one go.

'Thanks,' he replied simply.

After some time, when the stranger said to him, 'I had something to ask you for,' Amit asked loudly, 'what is it?'

'Can you give us in writing that you were a student of our coaching institute?'

Amit didn't understand and said, 'But I don't know anything about your institute. I never studied there, then why should I give it in writing?'

'Of course, you are right. But we will give you some money in return.'

The manager had the grace to look embarrassed and Malti walked over to them. She was curious about the newcomer and had not liked what she had heard. 'Money? What for, when we haven't done anything to do with your institute?'

The manager didn't want to respond to this question in front of everyone and said, 'You people celebrate, I will come some other day.'

*A mode of address for men used in Jabalpur to express fondness.

Shuklaji was a sharp man. It was his habit to hear every conversation keenly. He had understood everything by now. He said, 'Bhabhiji, this institute manager wants to use Amit's name. He will publicize the fact that Amit has secured the first position after studying in his institute. This will attract more students. This is what it is all about.'

Malti nodded but remained quiet. Although, Sunita, after thinking for a moment, said, 'This is not right.'

How could Kamla stay silent? She said, 'But what is wrong in his request? You are getting some money, just take it.'

Malti was smiling now and Amit was at a loss as to what was happening. Who doesn't want money? Anyhow, the desire for money was not in Malti's nature. Amit was still young, but he had stopped to think about it for a minute. He thought he would discuss this request with Guruji.

All of them were waiting for Guptaji. Malti told Usha, 'Why don't you distribute the sweets that the manager got?' Usha wanted Amit to have the first sweet, but Amit gave it to his mother.

Malti said softly, 'Beta, Didi too…'

When Amit fed Supriya with his own hands, everyone expressed their happiness by clapping their hands. Malti and Supriya had tears in their eyes and Aditi was happy seeing all this.

The very next day, Amit went to the school with Malti and spoke to Guruji about the manager and the institute. Guruji's experienced mind contemplated the future…if Amit has to study further, they will need money. Where will that come from? Preparing for medical entrance exams is costly. He thought, 'Maybe Amit should start taking tuitions. He will get money and all parents will want Amit to teach their children.' After considering all the possibilities Guruji advised, 'Speak to the coaching people. If Amit can teach there for an hour or two, they can pay him for that and whatever money he gets from it, he can use for his further studies.' Following Guruji's advice, Amit spoke to the institute's manager. What else could the manager ask for? He agreed instantly. That is how Amit started going to the institute from the following week.

The CBSE results were declared a few days later. Aditi too had passed her exams with very good grades. She had come first in her school with distinctions in all the subjects. Sunita was extremely happy and distributed sweets in the whole locality. Why shouldn't she express her joy? Aditi's achievement was, after all, the first success of her life.

18

AMIT had become the talk of the town. People from the neighbourhood and its vicinity were eager to send their children to him for studies. The school authorities had given him many rewards—medals, certificates, scholarship and some money. A function was also organized to felicitate Amit. Seeing the school being decorated for her own son, Malti, even after being told not to, had cleaned the school compound with vigour. Then most of the teachers and clerks had started telling her, 'Malti, you should stop doing this menial work now.' Another said, 'This doesn't become you.'

Malti would just smile at this. She had no false pride. Everyone knew that she was a quiet person and all of them were fond of her innocent and simple nature. Her habit of adjusting her saree's pallu to cover her head properly had become a part of her personality. The humility of a winner is appreciated—there was a difference in the way the world looked at her now, but Malti was unaware of this.

In the evening when the chairman and manager of the school management praised Amit lavishly, Malti had tears in her eyes. She, too, had been called to the stage to meet the chairman. He was praising them but had not refrained from appreciating his own school and the role of the management in Amit's success. Guruji then praised Amit's and Malti's efforts with a pure heart and had thanked God for Amit's achievement. On reaching home, Amit narrated all the events to Supriya, showing her all the garlands, certificates, trophies and money. All three of them were extremely happy; their life was suddenly filled with unexpected happiness. Since this family's aspirations and desires were very limited, their happiness was but natural.

When Amit began class XI, he studied even harder. He had been told that the class XII boards and the pre-medical test (PMT) were very difficult to crack. Going to the coaching institute in the evening, studying at night, long chats with Supriya—he didn't even realize when two whole years passed in this manner. He would meet Aditi every day as they studied at the same centre. Their schools, medium of study, books—all were different, but they would look at each other's books out of curiosity at times. They had both taken the XII board and PMT examinations and were now awaiting the results.

Amit used to share everything related to his studies with Aditi. Even though she was the same age, she was more mature than him. She would help him with more information, books, better atmosphere and various sources that she had access to. There was neither any enmity nor any love between them, just a great cooperation that could be called a close friendship. Amit had grown up into a young man now, with a beard and a moustache he'd left unshaved because he didn't know what to do about them. He was an extremely shy, emotional boy who was innocent in the ways of the world. He was not very confident, but was hardworking and intelligent. Similarly, Aditi had grown up into a young woman, but was not bothered about her looks—a black bindi, two plaits, and her hair soaked in oil. The trend of going to beauty parlours had not caught on then, but a few girls from the convent used to visit them. Aditi was considered backward and socially awkward in her class, but the glow of confidence could be seen on her face. She understood the world and its intricacies but was quite detached. She just wanted to be successful in her life, that was all. She was very smart, hardworking and sincere. Her mother had provided her with all facilities, but she wasn't too attached to them. She would come home straight after school and do nothing else but study. She spoke to everyone when the need arose, but was very fond of Malti and Supriya.

One night, a lot of people gathered in front of Amit's house.

The PMT results were out and Amit had secured the first position in that too. There was a festive atmosphere in the house. As earlier, Sonkar had already installed big speakers and today all the neighbours were dancing to the music, following the special tradition of Jabalpur. Reporters from all the local newspapers had reached Amit's house and since Malti had experienced all this before, she had made better arrangements this time. They had enough money now, in fact it was more than what they needed so she sent Sonkar's son, Raju, to get three kilos of laddoos and ordered tea from the neighbouring shop.

Amit's story was once again splashed on front pages of newspapers. By now, even he had become smarter and more mature. He didn't have too many friends and only a few classmates would visit to ask him something related to studies.

It was the day Aditi's results were to be announced too. Sunita was worried about Aditi and was agitated. The moment Aditi got a newspaper, she tried looking for her own roll number. She had started looking from the bottom and was getting worried as she had not found her roll number yet. There it was—she was delighted to spot it in the third line from the top. She jumped with joy and called out to her mother, 'Ma, even I have made it!'

'Great, even your name is there, beta!'

'Yes, Ma.'

Sunita had become emotional for the first time today. Her dream of all those years was coming true. Aditi ran into her mother's arms. Amit too forgot his own achievement and ran to Sunita and Aditi, saying, 'Congratulations, Aunty! Congratulations, Aditi!'

Aditi expressed her joy giving him a high five. Malti patted Aditi's shoulder and Supriya was calling out from inside.

The cameraman caught this image and the story of Aditi and Amit was published on the first page. One newspaper gave the headline: 'Diamonds amidst coal' while another said: 'Two doctors from a poor neighbourhood.' Somebody had even written:

'Education is not only for the rich.'

Amit was asked a lot of questions but he had the same answer: 'I want to study a lot.'

'Where will you go for further studies?'

'I will stay here, with my mother and sister.'

Somebody interrupted, 'He is the topper. He can study wherever he wants.'

The next morning dawned in a special way for both the families. Sunita distributed sweets to all the neighbours, all morning. In the afternoon, when Aditi whispered into her ears, 'Do tell Uncleji about this,' Sunita responded shyly, 'Why don't you tell him? He often asks about you.'

19

BY evening, Sethji had read the news in the papers and had come to the mohalla to visit them on his own. He was getting old now and was not physically very fit. On the other hand, the people from the neighbourhood had already started addressing Amit and Aditi as doctors. Most of the children referred to Amit as 'badde'. Now, Amit was a topic of discussion not only in his locality, Ghamapur Basti, but in the whole of Jabalpur and Madhya Pradesh. The MLA of the constituency, doctors from that area and even big institutions sent their congratulatory messages to Amit. And thus, the Darjani neighbourhood had become famous because of Amit. The coaching institute, too, had offered a lot of incentives to Amit and why wouldn't they? They were gaining in popularity because of Amit's association with them. The manager had made sure that the name of the institute was published in the newspapers with Amit's photographs for a few months as a professional move. The owner, manager and other teachers visited Amit's place regularly. He was their hero now and they wanted to sell his name as much as they could. Despite all the praise and attention showered on Amit, what was noteworthy was the fact that there was not even an iota of arrogance in him yet.

Guruji was extremely happy. He was quite old now and nearing retirement. He would often cite the example of Amit to his own children who were ordinary students. Guruji was never envious of Amit's success—instead, he was proud of him and always wished him well. He was one of the first people to reach Amit's place to congratulate him.

Amit's life had changed. He had started preparing for college with a single-minded sense of purpose. Even in his form, he had given first preference to the Jabalpur medical college. A few days back, he had even visited the campus with his friends, taking one of the mini buses that took passengers to the college which was at the other end of the town from the nearby Ghamapur crossing. Amit was quite excited to see the imposing building of the college. There was a commotion in the corridors—doctors in white aprons with stethoscopes, nurses in the wards and patients suffering from various ailments with their relatives attending to them—Amit had lost himself in all this. For a second, he felt he would get lost in this crowd. His house was quite far from the medical college, but the moment he reached there, his desire to study in the college took over.

Now he was waiting for the admission letter from the college. The postman knew the Darjani locality pretty well because he'd been busy bringing congratulatory letters to Amit. On one occasion, he had even asked Malti for a tip so she had given him some sweets.

Lalan was not far behind. One day, he too visited them on his bicycle—but to ask for a tip, not to supply milk. He had known Amit since childhood, so he showered his affection and blessings on him. Malti, too, had welcomed him with tea, snacks and sweets. Lalan was overcome with emotion.

Supriya's happiness was beyond expression. Her face was glowing and she felt a strange energy suffuse her body. But, the best effect was the ray of hope in her eyes. Her brother would become a doctor and treat her—and then, she would be able to lead a normal life. All three of them had envisioned this future together and now this dream was going to come true.

The day the PMT results were declared, Amit had gone to both the Hanuman and Durga temples—to make an offering of prasad for the first time, not to take some. When he looked at the idols, it seemed that the gods were smiling at him. Malti, too, had thanked the gods. The priest of the Hanuman temple knew Amit, who often used to sweep the temple premises and in return, the priest would offer him more prasad, which Amit always took home. Today, Malti had offered a kilo of laddoos which Amit and she had distributed to poor people at the temple. The hands that had always been lifted to receive were now raised in offering and there were tears in her eyes at the turn her life had taken.

The thought of the Durga and Hanuman temples brought Amit back to the present. There were tears in his eyes...how long had it been since he had visited a temple? The thought troubled him. Ma would always tell him to go there to ask for blessings from the deity—and he did, till he finished college. But for the past few years...in fact, he had not gone since Ma's death. He felt he had made a mistake. He would visit a temple once he was discharged from the hospital. But why would he? What was there in his life any more? What had the gods given him except for pain and sadness? He didn't remember doing anything wrong. Then why was he being punished? As far as Nikita was concerned, he had always supported her. But what did God give him in return? He didn't remember any instance where he was completely happy, he had always struggled with circumstances. Yet, the initial days of college were fun...

He opened his eyes and saw Aditi sitting on the sofa with her eyes closed. Akanksha was lying with her head on her lap. There was silence in the room. The ticking of the clock could be heard, but time passes without a sound. As soon as he closed his eyes, he was transported to the days gone by. He was remembering the first days of college. He had gone there for the first time with Aditi and that is where he had seen Nikita for the first time.

Section 3

20

AMIT received the call letter from the college on the same day as Aditi. Both of them were supposed to go to the college on a pre-decided date. Amit quickly scanned the letter with all its information and saw the amount that had to be paid as the fee. He was worried because he didn't have enough money, even though his earnings from teaching at the institute in the last two years had been saved in a bank because of Ma's foresight. He spoke to Guruji, who promised to provide for a part of the fees as a scholarship from the school. The coaching institute promised to pay the remaining amount, but got a five-year contract from Amit in return.

Aditi didn't have to worry about her fees. Sunita had spoken to Sethji who was delighted with Aditi's achievement. His own children were not very good at studies, but had started showing an interest in the family business. The frequency of his visits had come down because of his advancing age, but he had the same kind of authority over and love for both the families.

Malti was now a topic of discussion in the school. People would often tell her to give up her job and rest at home. Malti would only smile and say that they needed the money even more now as the college expenses were higher. Gita and Usha were with her in her happiness. Alka, too, was affectionate towards Amit and would often give him sound advice. However, Kamla's gibes continued, the main reason for which was jealousy. Her own children were no good at studies and therefore, Amit and Aditi had become irritants for her. As she usually did, she began to make barbed comments, this time as innuendos about the relationship between Amit and Aditi. Everyone knew her nature and ignored her.

On the insistence of his friends and Aditi, Amit agreed to

get two sets of shirts and trousers stitched. He already had shoes that he used in school and would continue using them in college as shoes were expensive. The quality of his clothes was slightly better than earlier and the local tailor had put in more effort in stitching them. Amit was now entering a new phase of life and his enthusiasm, naturally, was immense.

Ma had already visited the temples with Amit early in the morning on the first day of college. Sunita and Aditi were waiting for them. Sethji had sent a car, but Amit said, 'Aditi, you go in the car. I will take a tempo. I will have to take it from tomorrow onwards, anyway.' But, when Aditi and Sunita insisted, he hugged Supriya, kissed her on the forehead and went ahead to sit in a car for the first time in his life.

He was hesitant about getting into the car. He sat upright, clutching the door's handle. He was taken aback when the driver affectionately asked him to leave the handle, saying, 'The doors will open if you accidently turn it'. He got very worried the moment he heard this. He didn't even know that could happen! This was enough to make him feel embarrassed and inferior and he was sweating even though the weather was cool. He was seeing traffic on the road sitting on the front seat of the car for the first time. It felt as if the car was going to hit a bicycle any time. Each time a vehicle came too close to the car, he would shut his eyes in terror.

After this experience, once college began, Amit started avoiding other students because he realized that his background would be different from the others who came from the upper class. He didn't want to hide his poverty, but the ignorance about things richer people took for granted. His school friends knew him well and he was comfortable with them, but he was worried and scared about being in this new scenario, where he would meet people from all walks of life and different strata of society. He was aware of his disadvantages and this led to a lack of self-confidence in him, making him want to hide from the world. On the other hand, Aditi was brimming with confidence. She was used to being amongst people and knew how to handle them.

Amit had heard about the tradition of ragging in the first year, especially in medical colleges. He was very scared about this. On the first day, he was nervous seeing the college building. There was a crowd all around and he was afraid of getting lost in it. None of his school friends had been able to clear the medical entrance examination so the only people he knew were Sunita Aunty and Aditi. Avoiding all eyes and staring at the ground, he reached the administration block.

There were a lot of students there with somebody or the other accompanying them. Aditi was moving ahead, asking people for directions and Amit was following her. Just then he heard raised voices and saw that a man was shouting and arguing in the college office. Just when the office clerk was telling the man to go and meet the registrar, a gentleman was seen coming towards the office. The clerk stood up and said, 'Sir, this man is arguing with me for no reason.' The registrar understood the whole situation and was trying to explain things to the man but to no avail. A beautiful girl standing next to them interrupted and said, 'Let it be, Daddy.'

'No, these people need to understand. Where will I leave my daughter?'

'We have mentioned in our letter that we don't have enough rooms in the girls' hostel and you might need to make your own arrangements,' the registrar said, trying to explain.

'I will get somebody to call from Delhi. This is a government college—you can't do as you wish here. Do you think I am an idiot? Even I am a government officer,' the man said, seeming to be in the mood to fight.

'See, please understand that this is not my college. You are getting upset for no reason,' said the registrar patiently. 'It is a government college and the room will be allotted according to the rules. This may take a few days. You are the one in a hurry to get back; we can't help it if you cannot stay. We will wait for all the girls to whom call letters were sent and if any of them is higher on the merit list than your daughter and doesn't take a room, we will allot it to your daughter. Otherwise, you will have make other arrangements.'

The registrar left after explaining the situation but the father of the beautiful girl was not pacified. He was still mumbling and left only after a lot of insistence by his daughter. Amit glanced around and saw that there were more girls than he had expected. He had not spoken to too many girls before this as he had studied in a boys' school. He was shy of girls.

Aditi had tried a lot to persuade her mother not to accompany her to college, but Sunita was not one to listen. She went to college with Aditi again saying, 'Just for today...I will sit around and come back with you. I want to see how doctors study.' Amit reached college with Aditi, who found their classroom. The world seemed different to Amit today. All his confidence and enthusiasm about standing first was diminishing. He was a shy person to begin with and his circumstances had done little to boost his confidence. He had come from a small school and a poor family. When he entered the classroom, he saw that it was a big lecture hall with a lot of students dressed in modern, fashionable clothes. He looked at his own attire and the difference was remarkable. For a moment, he wanted to run away from there. Although, no one was looking at him, he felt as if all eyes were on him and he avoided looking at anyone. He was too young to understand that false ideas of superiority and inferiority are all in the mind.

The confident Aditi said to Amit, 'You sit on the other side; I will go and sit with the girls.'

She sat in the first row with the other girls and even started talking to some of them. Amit became even more nervous when he heard the girls talking in English with each other. He could not converse in English because he had never used it in everyday life although he could understand what was being said.

Aditi turned and looked at him as he hurriedly walked up the steps and sat in the last row. Sitting there he saw that all the boys were busy talking to each other. He was relieved that nobody was looking at him. The girls were making a lot of noise and the boys were excited to see them. Some of them had even started talking to the girls. He sat there, enjoying the scenario when suddenly an arm rested on his shoulders.

'Hi, I am Nema, Shyam Nema. And you?'

This was highly unexpected for Amit and he stood up saying, 'Yes s...ir, I am Amit.'

'Arre yaar, I am in the same class as you. I am not your senior. Sit, sit. Where are you from?' Nema asked, sitting next to him.

'From Jabalpur,' Amit replied as he sat down again.

'Oh, so badde, you are from Jabalpur.'

Hearing the word 'badde', Amit felt strangely comfortable. He knew this student must be from Jabalpur or some neighbouring area.

'I am from the nearby town of Narsinghpur, but I finished class XII from Jabalpur.'

Saying this, Nema inched closer to Amit; so close that Amit could smell tobacco from his mouth. Nema was munching on betel nuts, his simple, rustic behaviour and speech giving Amit some semblance of support.

'We own some land there. My father does farming, and we also have a shop there. What do your folks do?'

Nema was chewing on his betel and swallowing the juice as he could not spit it out in the classroom. Also, opening his mouth would reveal his red teeth. There were no signs of worry on his face as the ragging was yet to begin.

Amit lowered his eyes and answered, 'My father passed away when I was a child.'

'Oh, I am sorry, yaar.'

A sudden sadness flickered on Nema's face and both boys sat quietly for some time. Nema suddenly asked, 'Badde, are you the same Amit Saxena, the MP topper?'

'Yes.'

'Arre yaar, why didn't you tell me earlier? Brother, you are the studious type. You must have worked really hard.'

Amit could only manage a shy smile in response.

'Big brother, it's great to meet you.'

Amit, too, felt a strange affinity towards Nema who had made him feel comfortable. Amit glanced at Aditi while he talked to Nema. When looked in her direction this time, she saw that her seat was empty. Then, before he could wonder where she was, he saw her walking towards him.

'Are you all right?'

Amit stood up hurriedly and said, 'Yes, yes.'

'Okay, I am sitting there,' she said, pointing to her seat. 'Let me know if you need me.' Aditi returned to her seat.

Shyam Nema asked naughtily, 'Big brother, now who is that?'

'She is my neighbour.'

Nema rolled his eyes and said, 'That is great...'

Amit found his behaviour strange but stayed quiet. Nema was looking around, seeing all the smart, beautiful girls who were sitting in pretty clothes. He was in a mood for pranks and asked, 'Who do you think is the prettiest of them all, leaving your neighbour aside?'

Amit lowered his gaze shyly.

'Oh yaar, look at those three girls. How amazing!'

Amit looked at them surreptitiously at Nema's insistence... Nema is right, thought Amit...they are so beautiful. The three girls sitting away from the others were talking amongst themselves. Their way of talking and clothes made it evident that they were not from this city. One of them was the girl whose father had been fighting in the dean's office earlier. That girl's beauty was incomparable, with her fair complexion, long black tresses, oval face, playful eyes and shapely neck. Her features and make-up reminded one of Khajuraho, as if the statues had come alive in modern clothes...Amit wanted to look at her again and again, unable to stop his eyes from wandering in her direction.

A smart boy came towards Nema and patting his shoulder said, 'Hello, guys!'

Nema gave him his hand quickly saying, 'Hello!'

'I am Vikram—Vicky, from Delhi.'

'I am Shyam Nema from Narsinghpur.'

'Where is this Narsinghpur, yaar?'

'It's right here, near Jabalpur.'

'Oh and you, doctor sahib?' Vikram asked, pointing towards Amit.

'I am Amit from Jabalpur.'

'So brother, what is going on in your city...?' Vikram said, making himself comfortable in the chair.

Then Shyam said, 'This is Amit, the MP PMT topper,' taking the conversation further.

Vikram did not seem to hear as his eyes were fixed on the row of girls. Staring at them, he said, 'Arre yaar, there are too many students in this class. Why are you sitting at the back? Let's go to the front.'

'Brother, we are fine here,' Nema said informally, without paying much attention to him. Amit had again retreated into his shell. Vikram's arrival had made him uncomfortable. His attractive personality, expensive clothes and broad frame were enough to bring back his sense of inferiority.

The noise in the classroom rose to a crescendo, but suddenly there was a hush. The dean and other professors had come in, their air of authority quietening the students down.

21

REMEMBERING his old college days made Amit restless. The light of early dawn was filtering into the hospital room. Light was waking the world up, but the darkness of night refused to go away from his heart. He looked around to distract himself from the thoughts and memories that troubled him, but saw that Aditi was not there. Akanksha had woken up, but was leaning with her head on the wall. Her eyes were closed and face calm, only her breathing showing that she was alive. He could hear the ward boys and maids cleaning the ward. Even though this was a government hospital, it was clean and hygienic. Lying down in these familiar surroundings, where he lived and worked, Amit felt some peace, even though he was a patient now. Then he began to worry about Nikita. When one is physically sick, the heart becomes more cowardly and the mind is prone to distractions. Often, old memories come to the mind and because one is lying inert, the next step is to analyze them.

Memories flit by the mind, either filling the mind with regret or evoke pleasant associations, rather like being part of an audience watching a film with a certain detachment. Falling into the same trap, Amit went back to his past...

Nikita's beautiful, innocent face in their college days came into focus in his mind's eye...Vikram, Amit and Shyam, though not really friends, had become a group. Aditi used to speak to both the boys because of Amit and Nikita and her acquaitance Radhika knew Vikram because they were from Delhi. Thus, Aditi, Nikita and Radhika had also become a group. It was not as if there was much friendship amongst them too. Radhika had got a hostel room on the first day and Nikita, too, had got one on the second day because of the temporary allotment of a few rooms of the nursing hostel for undergraduate female students. Radhika had shifted in with Nikita. Radhika was a simple and quiet girl, whereas, Nikita was smart, attractive and eloquent and just like her father, Nikita was always in a hurry. One meeting was enough to understand that her father was a very shrewd man—proving himself right always and believing himself to be the smartest. Being from the same city, Delhi, Nikita, Radhika and Vikram had developed a good understanding. Vikram had made friends with Nikita even before her father had left. He, too, was quite shrewd.

'...Uncle, you don't need to worry. If we will not look after each other, being from the same city, who else will? We can even travel to Delhi together. And as far as the hostel is concerned, Nikita has already got a room and Radhika is with her. We will manage everything.'

Within a few minutes, Vikram had won Nikita's father's heart by introducing himself. Since Vikarm belonged to a business family who owned a bungalow in south Delhi, Mr Sood, Nikita's father, was quite impressed. Vikram introduced him to Amit and Shyam too, to show off his group. Aditi too was standing nearby... Amit remembered clearly...that group that was formed in the initial days of college lasted till almost the end. Vikram had easily attracted Nikita and Amit noticed that Mr Sood's behaviour with Vikram was amiable, whereas it was barely civil with the others.

Vikram had rented a room outside the college, in Shastri Nagar because the hostel rooms were too small for him. Shyam stayed in the hostel, like many other boys. It was an old government college, about thirty to forty years old and the hostel was quite dilapidated, but it was too expensive to stay outside. In the hostel, they could spend time with friends and the mess food did not taste that bad.

Amit and Aditi used to travel to college together almost everyday in the same tempo. Once Amit was humiliated and beaten up by the seniors of the hostel when they had got to know that he was the topper. He felt as if he had committed a crime. He had paid the price for his innocence and simple-mindedness. His silence had been mistaken for arrogance, which had led to a few more slaps. When he was made to take off all his clothes, he felt he would die of shame...and when he was made to wear his undergarments over his clothes, he had broken into bitter tears. His poverty was evident from his torn underwear, which had been concealed by his clothes. He had never faced violence before and the first slap of his life stunned him.

His mother was distraught when she saw his face all swollen up. He had calmed down only when Aditi managed to convince him that ragging would last only for a few more days. The seniors teased him, linking him with Aditi, and this was the reason why he had started avoiding her. He would go straight to class immediately after getting off the tempo or bus, but Adiit would still try to accompany him.

On the other hand, Vikram took good care of Nikita and Radhika from the very first day. Shyam had become very fond of Amit and Vikram liked both of them. This group of six would be together in the practicals sessions, in the canteen, the coffee house and the library. Whether it was the canteen, the coffee house or Jain hotel's strong tea, Shyam would always pay for Amit. The hostel tea was just not good enough, tasting like ditch water. Shyam often went to the hotels across the road to have his paan after a session of ragging. Amit would refuse to go but Shyam insisted on taking him along.

For Nikita, Jabalpur was a small, backward town and she would often make fun of it. Vikram agreed to everything that she said. It had become his habit to make her wish his command. In this group of six, three were from Jabalpur and three from Delhi, but it was Nikita's view that everyone had to agree to. Jabalpur is a smaller town as compared to Delhi and perhaps provincial, but Aditi resented Nikita's criticism of her hometown. The two would often argue, but Nikita always won. Vikram would support her so Aditi had to give up after a while.

Amit was a young man now but was oblivious to romantic relationships and the flirting game. Aditi was one of the most popular girls. Even though she dressed simply, she was beautiful. The seniors troubled her a lot in the initial days, but she ignored them as she was interested only in her studies. By the time they reached the second semester, people had stopped noticing her because she did not encourage any attention.

On the other hand, Nikita was the most attractive girl in the class and liked to wear fashionable clothes. She had become a topic of discussion in the first semester itself, but her aggressive and volatile behaviour scared all the boys off. That was also the reason why she had been ragged less severely. All of them tried various ploys to get her attention, but none of them could succeed and then, Vikram was always following her like a shadow. Vikram escaped ragging because he did not stay in the hostel and his confidence and carefree personality protected him. He, too, was a topic of discussion in the whole college along with Nikita. Vikram roamed around on his motorcycle with Nikita most of the time. They would go out of the city, watch movies, have dinner outside—this had become a daily routine by the second semester. When Vikram, Nikita and Radhika travelled to Delhi together for the summer holidays, he spent the journey looking after Nikita and talking only to her, while Radhika spent all the time staring outside the window. He had not even asked Radhika if she wanted a glass of water. But that didn't bother Radhika much, but she later told Shyam that Vikram had visted Nikita at her place several times at Delhi.

Shyam Nema belonged to a family of zamindars. As soon as ragging got over he got his scooter to the college and went to Bhedaghat along with Radhika, Nikita and Vikram. They had a lot of fun boating in the Narmada river at this spot about fifteen to twenty kilometres outside the city and marvelling at the imposing marble rocks on the banks. They had asked Amit and Aditi to come along but Amit refused because Sunday was the only day he could go to the coaching institue and earn some money by giving tuitions. College had led to an increase in his expenses.

Shyam reported to him after returning, 'Vikram and Nikita have become quite close to each other.'

Nikita's behaviour was aggressive. She would get extremely angry at the slightest provocation. She would raise a hue and cry if the food was not to her liking. One day, she fought without any reason with Radhika regarding the cleanliness of the room. At first, Radhika tried to reason with her, but had to clean the entire room when Nikita refused to listen. This incident had left Radhika very troubled—she had not been able to pay attention in class all day, but Nikita remained unaffected.

'Why do you listen to her? If it is that difficult, why doesn't she stay in another room? It is her responsibility, too, to clean the room,' Aditi said in plain simple words, but Radhika did not respond.

Nikita had gone for breakfast to the coffee house with Vikram, not bothering about Radhika. When Shyam got to know in the afternoon that Radhika had not eaten anything since morning, he took her to the canteen and forced her to eat. This was the beginning of their closeness and the two formed a relationship destined to last. The announcement of their engagement in the last semester had caught Amit and Aditi by surprise. Radhika and Shyam had kept up the dignity and stability of their relationship till the end whereas, Nikita and Vikram had become famous as an attractive couple who disregarded all boundaries.

Nikita had started frequenting Vikram's flat. This was a topic of discussion in the college initially, but later people accepted the fact. She spent most of her time roaming around with Vikram but took Amit's help in studies and asserted her right over him. Amit would often have to do her practicals for clinical tests and ended up writing her notes too. And if he refused to do it, she would argue for hours. This didn't bother Vikram. He trusted Amit and Shyam and therefore, had no problems if Nikita spoke to them. But, he did not like it if anyone else spoke to her. Vikram, however, was not allowed to speak to any other girl as Nikita could not bear that.

Vikram did not want really want to be tied down. But, because of Nikita's cantankerous behaviour, he did not talk to other girls in front of her. Maybe, he didn't want to lose her or was scared of her! But, when he became a senior, he would tease attractive junior girls and even meet them and talk to them secretly.

Amit and Shyam found themselves forced to cover up for Vikram, who would ask them to give him an alibi after a fight with Nikita. She would not believe Vikram's denials when confronted by her, until Amit said that Vikram did not meet or speak to anyone. Amit often contemplated telling the truth to Nikita, but did not as he was scared of her.

Amit had had to work very hard since the beginning of his medical studies. He had studied in Hindi medium in school, and English was proving to be a difficulty here. Slowly, with a lot of grit, he had succeeded in understanding enough of the language for his studies, but could not use it in conversation. Nikita would often make fun of him for this and that intensified the feeling of inferiority in him. However, his diligence had already been noticed by the professors and senior doctors. His intelligence overshadowed all his weaknesses. He was everyone's favourite—straightforward and helpful. And Nikita often took advantage of this when she bunked practicals or played hookey as the professors trusted Amit and would believe him when he covered for her. Even Amit did not know why he did this for her—maybe out of a sense of duty as a friend and because they were part of a group.

One day, towards the end of the first semester, Nikita was caught by the laboratory attendant. He was anyway upset with her behaviour and on one occasion had gone around muttering, 'What does she think of herself? Even doctors don't speak to me like this...now she will teach me how to keep the lab clean...why does she want to become a doctor if she can't stand the smell of formelene?...Let her complain against me and then let us see how she becomes a doctor.'

Shyam and Vikram handled the situation, calming the attendant, but one day, when Nikita was particularly rude, he complained to the anatomy professor.

The anatomy professor was very strict and summoned Nikita and Vikram to see him and give him their explanation the next day. Amit too was called as he was responsible for the proxy attendance that he had done for Nikita. Amit was very scared, but there was no sign of worry on Nikita's and Vikram's faces. Amit was amazed to see this, wondering how someone else could make a mistake, have their fun and get him punished for it! On Shyam's insistence, Amit told the professor that Nikita had not attended the class in the lab because she was scared of corpses. The professor had let Nikita go because of Amit but Vikram had to spend several days in the anatomy hall with the corpses as a punishment.

This pattern continued in the next semester in pathology and gynaecology clinical labs. Vikram and Nikita had pleaded with Amit and got their work done, but he had refused to do this in the surgery clinical lab as the professor, nurse and lab attendant were all strict in that department.

22

SHYAM was busy studying preventive medicine in the second semester. He had taken a room outside the hostel and this had increased his responsibilities. Exams too were approaching. He was studying with Amit in the library when Nikita stormed in looking for Vikram. Shyam responded teasingly, 'How would we know? We thought he was with you.'

'Shyam, I am not in the mood for jokes. I hope you did not see him with some girl.'

'How would we see him?'

His tone made Nikita even more angry and when Shyam saw that she was furious, he asked, trying to calm her down, 'What happened?'

'I don't know. I haven't seen him since morning.'

Just then, Shyam saw Vikram and heaved a sigh of relief, 'Here he comes.'

'Where were you? Who were you having fun with?' Nikita turned and shouted at Vikram.

A storm seemed to have hit the library and everyone turned to stare at them. Vikram held her by the shoulders and said smilingly, 'Speak softly. Everyone is looking at us.'

'Why? You don't seem to have any shame anyway, where were you since morning?' she asked even more loudly.

Vikram looked around—people were staring at him sharply. When Shyam asked both of them to go out and talk, Nikita said in an irritated voice, 'Please don't interrupt, Shyam. I am talking to Vicky.'

'Okay, let us go out and talk,' Vikram held her by the hand and took her to the corridor. They argued for a long time, but finally, Vikram succeeded in calming her down.

He looked a little hassled when he came to the coffee house in the evening. After some time he said on his own, 'She is too sharp, man, she is like a dictator. She just can't talk nicely, fights about everything. At times I feel like I am meeting some headmistress of a school and not my girlfriend. I am not a bonded labourer. There has to be some freedom in relationships...but she wants to keep me in shackles. No one gets tied down like this, anyway, forget it...I managed to save myself today.' There was both anger and revolt in his words.

Nikita would have a fight with someone or the other every third or fourth day. People got attracted to her beautiful face but were repelled by her rudeness and therefore, she didn't have any friends. Radhika was with her by virtue of being her roommate and because she was from the same city. Shyam was her friend because of Radhika. Nikita asserted her right over Amit in such a way that he could not refuse to give in to her and Aditi was a part of this group only because of Amit, otherwise she did not like Nikita much. Radhika told everyone that even Nikita's father was very short-tempered. She said that Nikita's mother had once told her, 'I know my daughter, like her father, has a temper, but then, she is our youngest child and a little spoilt. What can we do, dear? She is a little stubborn.'

Amit remembered...at times Nikita would be extremely happy and talk animatedly, but on other occasions she would fall strangely silent. Whenever she was quiet, people thought that she had had a fight with Vikram. Radhika would tell them that Nikita was an insomniac and at times she had had to stay up with her.

Vikram had become quite notorious in the college for not being serious about studies and he would get a supplementary in every semester. Amit, Aditi, Radhika and Shyam were performing quite well, but Nikita passed with much difficulty. Before every result, Shyam would tease Vikram, 'How many Julys are you getting this time?'

'Arre, what is this July?' Nikita had asked with an amused expression.

'It is a name for a supplementary.'

'Oh,' she said and smiled.

Vikram, sitting nearby, was smiling too.

'This is what will happen if you don't study. Anyway, Vikram need not worry. He is the son of a rich father. He will earn much more than all of us by opening a hospital once he becomes a doctor,' Aditi said, trying to tease him.

'Who is stopping you from earning money? Yes, but how will you do that in this small town—Jabalpur? The poor can't pay much. Delhi is a different story. It is a big city with rich people…' Nikita interrupted. She did not like it even if someone said something as a joke to Vikram.

Vikram tried to handle the situation and said, 'I will not live in Delhi. I will go abroad. What will one do in India?'

'And what about me?' Nikita asked, looking at Vikram with anger in her eyes.

'You too come along. Let your father know.'

'Why my father?'

'Because your father is the one who will arrange for your further studies. What can I do regarding that?' Vikram said this simply but Nikita got even more enraged and walked away muttering to herself. However, this time Vikram did not follow her.

'Where will you go, Mr Topper?' Vikram asked Amit. This was the first time he had not paid any attention to Nikita. However, Amit was watching Nikita go away and he replied without thinking, 'I don't know.'

Amit often found Vikram and Nikita's behaviour strange. He always felt that Vikram's behaviour towards Nikita was not satisfactory. Then he wondered why he even bothered to think about their relationship. Was this because he had a soft corner for Nikita? And if yes, why was that so? He himself didn't know but he had not expressed this feeling ever. Nikita's behaviour didn't bother him. According to him, her screaming and shouting was always Vikram's fault. He wanted Nikita to be happy and that is why helped her whenever she asked for his help in studies and slowly, Nikita had become completely dependent on Amit for her notes and lab practicals.

In the third semester, Amit saw Vikram roaming around with a girl from the first semester and mentioned this to Shyam. Shyam responded saying, 'What can we do? Nikita will not believe us if we tell her. On the contrary, she will get angry with us. Just keep quiet.'

When Amit asked Radhika, she sounded a little worried, 'One just can't tell. At times, she is very happy and at others she becomes absolutely quiet. But, she comes back to the hostel late every night. The warden too is upset with her. They have even complained to her family in Delhi. I don't know what happened, but it seems that her family knows and is okay with this. Maybe, Nikita and Vikram are planning to get married.'

'When are they getting married?' Shyam asked excitedly.

'I don't know but it seems that Vikram is not in a hurry and Nikita is. That is why they fight every day. I think there is a problem...why don't you guys talk to Vikram?'

Shyam and Amit were sitting at the coffee house in the evening whem Vikram came in smiling. 'What is the matter? You seem very happy. It looks like you didn't get a scolding today. But how will you manage after marriage?' Shyam said jokingly.

'Marriage? Whose marriage?' Vikram stopped for a minute before sitting on the chair.

'Yours. Who else's?'

'With whom?'

'With Nikita. Who else?'

'Am I crazy...?' There was a sharpness in Vikram's scornful laughter.

'Then what is it between the two of you?' Amit said as he was unable to stop himself. Nikita's lovely face came before his eyes.

'What's between the two of us? We are good friends. We like each other, like to roam around together and that is what we do. As far as marriage is concerned, I have not thought about it.'

Vikram winked while saying this. Amit felt almost nauseous due to a surge of emotion. 'Is this even possible? Vikram should not cheat on her.' On the other hand, Shyam gave Vikram a high five and both laughed loudly.

Amit had started feeling a strange affection for Nikita since then. Most probably, it was out of sympathy. He could not bear to see anyone close to him in pain. He started asking after her and tried taking care of her. Several times he felt that he should warn Nikita about Vikram, but what right did he have to speak? In the end, he managed to ask only this much, 'I hope you are fine.'

Nikita would always respond in an irritated manner, 'Yes, yes, I am fine.'

Sometimes she would smile or in the extreme, stay absolutely silent. Her silence troubled Amit. How different was this Nikita from the one who he had met in the first semester. Maybe, roaming around and eating out had made her gain a lot of weight. There was another difference that the others in the group had noticed—these days, Nikita would often be seen running after Vikram who didn't pay much attention to her any more.

23

To get a proper medical education, even twenty-four hours a day for three hundred and sixty-five days are not enough. There is barely any time to nurture relationships or do anything else. It is true that by increasingly advanced knowledge, the medical sciences have gained victory over several diseases, but science does not have all the answers. An attempt to understand human beings can take several lifetimes. Life science can have no control over the feelings and lifestyle of human beings. It can examine, understand, and to an extent, treat the human body. But, it cannot control emotions and the soul.

One day, Amit was alone in Shyam's flat. He would stay at Shyam's to study as commuting to and from home took a lot of time. It was convenient to go to the library too this way. Since he was put on night duty in the last semester, it was not possible to go home every night. He had just started studying the characteristics of the heart's artery when he heard a loud knock at the door. Shyam had said he would return late with Radhika. How had he returned so early?

He opened the door and was bewildered at the sight before him. A dishevelled Nikita was standing at the door. Her hair hung untidily on her shoulders and her clothes were in disarray. Her expression conveyed volumes, showing something really bad had happened, and tears were flowing from her eyes. She looked at Amit for an instant and walked into the room. She sat down heavily on the chair and began crying bitterly. Amit did not know what to do. He could not gather the courage to hold her and stop her from crying. He could only ask, 'What happened?'

Nikita was not in a condition to say anything. It seemed that she would swoon and fall down. Amit got very worried and asked loudly, 'Will you tell me what happened?' Nikita looked at him with blank eyes.

'Vikram...'

'What happened to Vikram?' Amit screamed. He was worried that something bad had happened to his friend.

'Nothing has happened to him. He is your friend, right?' she said softly in between sobs. She kept wiping off her tears mechanically and when Amit did not answer, she took his hand in hers and asked again, '...he is your friend, right?'

The confused Amit managed to shake his head and say, 'Yes.'

'Then why don't you make him understand?' she said, pulling at his collar. Then she hid her face in her palms.

'What is there to explain? He is what he is. He is not worthy of you, just leave him.'

Amit didn't know how the words had come out. He wanted to say a lot more, but on hearing this, Nikita stopped crying and said agitatedly, 'Why? I have been with him all these years. How can I leave him like this? And I can't do it even more so now... why don't you understand?' Anger had replaced her tears.

'What should I understand?' Amit was getting irritated now. What could he do about their relationship? He knew what Vikram was like but how could he explain it to Nikita?

'I have reached a situation where I cannot leave him.'

'So, don't leave him. What is the problem? But what has happened now?' Amit said, adjusting his shirt and moving towards a chair.

'He pushed me out of the house. He says I should get an abortion done.'

'What?'

Amit stood fixed to the spot. He turned and looked at Nikita. His ears had gone numb. He was not in a condition to hear anything else. He held the arms of the chair so tightly that, it could have given way. There was surprise on his face and anger was brewing in his veins. How could this happen? He could not believe it. If it was someone else, he could have said, 'It is your fault, what can I do? You should see what to do.' Maybe, he would have blamed both of them. But as of now, Amit was very angry at Vikram. Why was his reaction so intense? Was it that there was an undefinable bond with the others just by virtue of studying with them for all these years? Maybe...but he did not have time for an answer to this now. As of now, the only question in his mind was, 'How could Vikram do this?'

Nikita seemed even more beside herself. She had stopped speaking but her eyes were lowered and seemed to need support. Amit himself was in a daze. Strong emotions made him almost helpless.

He said with difficulty, 'Where is Vikram right now?'

There was no response from Nikita.

'You stay here. I will go and speak to him.' Amit was angry now. Within a minute, he was out of the door and started towards Vikram's house without thinking.

Radhika and Shyam reached home some time after Amit had left and were startled to see Nikita alone there, still crying.

'Nikita! What happened? Where is Amit?'

After asking her several times, Nikita said while crying bitterly, 'He has gone to Vikram's place and...'

Nikita looked at Radhika and fainted. It seemed that she had been waiting for her. Radhika and Shyam both were very worried. They checked Nikita's pulse. It was very fast. They sprinkled some water on her face, but to no avail. Her pain was evident from her face. Radhika took off Nikita's slippers and made her lie on the bed. Shyam took in a long breath and closed his eyes. Then he left the room, picked up his scooter and left for Vikram's place, leaving Radhika with Nikita.

The sun had gone down. It was dark now and was becoming increasingly difficult to recognize people on the street. Shyam was trying to see the faces of all the passers-by. He was constantly thinking—what had happened? Was Vikram all right? Had he met with an accident? Jabalpur's traffic is horrible and he drives very fast. But, if he had, Nikita would have been with him. I hope she didn't see him with another girl...but why would Amit go to Vikram's place in that case? He is not one to leave his studies in the middle...Shyam Nema was trying to see the people on the road in the light of his flashlight while thinking about all this and it felt as if his head would burst.

Meanwhile, Amit was moving angrily towards Vikram's house. He didn't know what he was going to say or do. Right now, he was just plain angry.

Amit reached Vikram's place and rang the doorbell. Vikram opened the door and said smilingly, 'Arre, Badde, how come you are here so late at night?'

'What is all this?' Amit fumed.

'What is what?' Vikram replied simply.

'With Nikita...' Amit could not speak much because his anger was becoming uncontrollable now.

'What happened to Nikita?' Vikram was still talking in a calm manner.

Now Amit held him by the shoulders and shook him, 'Do you think what you are doing is right?'

This caught Vikram by surprise but he responded by removing Amit's hands from his shoulders strongly, 'Who are you to speak between the two of us? It is our personal matter.'

'Even I want this to remain your personal matter. Come on, let's go and get you married to her.' Emotions overcome practicality and Amit had said this quite automatically.

'Look Amit, let us not take this any further. I will never get married to that mad girl. Yes, I am willing to bear all the expenses. I had said this to her too, but she is a smart girl, she wants to trap me. I agree we have had a lot of fun together but she, too, was a part of it out of her own accord. I had never promised marriage. She was enjoying herself till now, why all this suddenly?' Vikram was a strong guy, he still had control over himself and he meant what he was saying.

Shyam had reached Vikram's flat by then. Not knowing what they were arguing about, he tried to make peace between them. He asked, 'Amit, Vikram, what is the matter? Nikita is lying unconscious at my place...'

'So? What should I do? Hang that sick, crazy woman around my neck and kill myself? I have understood her now. I will never do what she wants. She has already created a huge scene here. Next time, I am going to let people see what happens. I am not scared of the police or the court.'

'You will not call her crazy in this condition,' Amit screamed, raising his voice probably for the first time in his life.

But this did not affect Vikram in any way. Probably, all his feelings for Nikita had waned by now. He pushed Amit out and said, 'There is no need to shout, do you understand? I have been respecting our friendship, otherwise I would have broken your hands and legs by now. If you care for her this much, why don't *you* get married to her? She will show you heaven, but later when she will come to bite you, then you will understand.'

Shyam pulled Amit out of the flat and did not say anything to Vikram, seeing how angry he was. He still wasn't clear about what exactly had happened.

Amit left Vikram's place defeated. His anger had drained and he was feeling very weak. After some time, Shyam himself said, 'Everything will be fine. Let Vikram's anger die down. Even Nikita needs to lead a normal life. You can't always be in war mode.'

Amit did not respond. Radhika was waiting for them at home, 'Where were you both? I have been waiting. Nikita is under a lot of stress. She is bleeding. Maybe we will have to...abort...'

'Is there no chance of saving the pregnancy?'

'No'

'Are you sure?'

'Quite sure.'

'Then it won't be wise to take her to the hospital,' Amit said with authority. He was full of sympathy for Nikita and anger had been replaced by his feelings for her.

'But where is Vikram?'

'You wait here. We need to bring all the instruments here itself. What do you think, Shyam?' Amit avoided the question raised by Radhika.

'Yes, you are right.' Shyam had understood everything in an instant and stood there bewildered.

24

THE entire bed and Nikita's clothes were soiled. Shyam and Amit had brought a dilator and other medical equipment, from the hospital. They had also brought essential medicines and anaesthesia along. Amit assisted Radhika as she proceeded to clean up Nikita. She was still under shock.

When it was over, Amit washed his hands covered in blood. When he returned to the room, he drew in long breaths. Nikita was staring into nothingness. He went close to her and stroked her forehead to show her that she was not alone. He had never even dreamt that he would see Nikita in this condition ever. There was silence all around. He was feeling like a criminal—a friend, whom he had observed from such close quarters, who used to be stubborn and often asserted her right over him—a friend he had not been able to help.

Shyam came in and said, 'Everything will be all right. Things like this do happen. Amit tried...but...you don't worry...'

His words had no effect on Nikita and she continued staring blankly at the wall. Amit sat next to her, helpless. Shyam walked out into the balcony and Radhika had fallen asleep sitting on one of the chairs outside the room.

It was 3 a.m., the dark night had passed stealthily. Sleep was overcoming Amit and Shyam too but Nikita's stony eyes refused to give way.

On hearing the chirping of birds, Amit woke up. As he saw Shyam stirring, he said, 'We should tell him. What he wanted has been done. Let us see what he wants now.' Shyam agreed but stopped Amit from going to Vikram's house. Radhika woke up when she heard the two friends whisper. It was still early in the morning when Shyam set out for Vikram's flat, filled with hope.

But barely ten minutes had passed and he was back. Radhika was surprised. She asked, 'What happened? Is Vikram coming?'

'No.'

'What did he say?' Radhika was still hopeful.

'He has gone mad, says he is not interested and that it's all over.'

Radhika's face fell as she heard this. Shyam had spoken softly, but his words reached the room inside. Amit sat transfixed on the stool next to the bed. Nikita had turned her face away and lay with her back to him. Amit got up and as he took her hands in his, he said, 'Be strong'.

Nikita started weeping bitterly. She clutched Amit's hand, sobbing loudly. Hearing her, both Shyam and Radhika came rushing inside. Shyam was teary-eyed seeing Nikita break down and Radhika also wept silently, stroking her friend's forehead.

25

SHYAM and Amit went to college that day with a heavy heart while Radhika stayed with Nikita to look after her. Shyam applied for leave for both of them. In the third and last semester, there are more clinicals and less non-clinical and lecture classes. Whether it is surgery or gynaecology, students have to go to the ward, hospital and operation room for clinical practice. Going to the maternity ward implied the gynaecology lab. That day they had a class in the maternity ward for the gynaecology clinical. The moment the doctor started talking about the first case study, Amit was reminded of Nikita's abortion. It seemed as if blood was still sticking to his hands. His eyes were constantly going towards his palms. The next moment he felt very anxious. He felt a strange ache in his heart and when he could not concentrate, he came out of the ward. He could see Nikita's face in every woman's face. When he couldn't bear it, he went home and lay down on his bed, trying to sleep.

Ma and Supriya both could not understand what had happened. This was the first time Amit had returned from college and had not spoken to anyone. Usually, he would not rest till he had spoken to both Supriya and Ma. Even if he had a lot of studies to do, he would sit next to Supriya and start studying only after having tea. Today, Malti saw that there was sadness and fatigue on her son's face. She touched his forehead, but he didn't have fever. Finally, she asked him, 'What happened, beta? Are you feeling all right?'

'Yes, I am fine. I just want to rest,' he said and turned to the other side, trying to sleep. Seeing her mother get worried, Supriya looked at her brother with surprise in her eyes.

Radhika stayed at Shyam's place for two or three days to look after Nikita. She didn't mind staying with Shyam anyway as the date of their engagement had been fixed. Forgetting that they were living together for the first time, they looked after Nikita with great care. Shyam suggested that Nikita should go home for a few days. But when Radhika mentioned this to her, she did not answer but just enquired about Amit. Radhika and Shyam both were sensible and knew it was not wise to send her alone in her condition. Radhika could not accompany her as both she and Shyam had to prepare for the engagement. Finally, Radhika suggested, 'Ask Amit, he might go...but why hasn't he come for the past two days?'

Shyam went to Amit's place that evening. Amit had still not recovered from the trauma of the incident. The moment he saw Shyam he asked, 'How is she?'

'She stays very quiet, doesn't say anything. She was asking about you. I was telling her to go home, to Delhi. But she just doesn't talk. She should go, it will be a good change. Maybe, she doesn't want to go alone. Radhika and I can't go, so it will be good if you can go with her.'

'Possibly, she doesn't want to face her parents. Let us send her a little later. Anyway, I will come tomorrow.'

The next morning when Amit reached Shyam's place, Radhika asked, 'Where have you been? Nikita has been asking about you.'

'Where is she?'

'In the balcony at the back. She is not talking. Let us take her to the college. It will be a good change,' said Radhika, worried about her.

Nikita was standing in the balcony staring at the sky. The girl who was always talking loudly, had nothing to say today. The playful face was sad. Her dishevelled hair was proof that she had been unable to sleep.

'How are you?' Amit tried smiling at her, leaning on the railing of the balcony. But he had not been able to say anything more as she did not respond. However, he did look at her face from time to time.

'Come, lets us go to the college. Have a bath, freshen up.'

There was love and concern in Amit's voice.

The eyes that had been staring into nothingness turned to him. When Amit looked deep into them, he saw an emptiness there. Radhika came in and broke the silence and after a lot of pleading from her, Nikita bathed and went to college with them.

She sat in the coffee house for some time. Radhika and Shyam had left after having coffee. Amit wanted to go to class, but he saw Vikram approaching lightheartedly. The moment Nikita saw him, she clenched her fists and anger seeped into her eyes. Without looking at her, Vikram sat on a table far away. Nikita held Amit's hand tightly and almost pulled him outside the coffee house.

'Running away like this won't work. Face him and if he doesn't have any feelings, why do you care?' Amit said.

Nikita walked towards the hostel without uttering a word. On reaching the hostel gate, Amit said softly, 'Go home, go to Delhi for a few days.'

The despondent Nikita just managed to say, 'Thank you' with tears in her eyes. Then she turned and went inside swiftly.

26

ADITI was a mature girl. She was both sensible and practical. She was not concerned about anything other than her goal—to become a doctor. The fact that Amit and Nikita were spending more time together didn't disturb her, but she was surprised. On seeing both of them so quiet, she had even asked Shyam and Radhika if something had happened, but both had averted the discussion by saying, 'nothing important.'

Seeing Vikram's flirtatious behaviour, intelligent girls stayed away from him but those of the same temperament enjoyed his company. Vikram spent most of his time having fun with such girls and if nothing else, flirted with trainee nurses. For him it was one and the same thing if a girl was attracted to him swayed by emotions or because she was needy, and it was not difficult to get momentary love by using some money. Often, Vikram would go to the city to enjoy himself.

He didn't know much about Aditi, but he tried his luck with her too. Annoyed, Aditi gave him a piece of her mind, but true to his shamelessness, he left smiling.

One day, when Aditi saw Amit alone, she asked him, 'What is the matter? I don't get to see you, don't you come to college regularly? Is everything okay at home? And what is wrong with Nikita these days...why does she stay away from Vikram? One day Vikram said something improper to me too...what is the matter?'

'No, no, it's nothing,' he swiftly avoided Aditi's questions.

'Okay, I will come home one of these days. Tell Aunty that I was asking about her. How is Supriya? Give her my love.'

For a year or so, Aditi was living with her mother in a rented house near college. Ghamapur was far from there and a lot of time got wasted in travelling.

'And yes, be careful. Don't get into a deep friendship with people like Nikita and Vikram. Do whatever you do, but thoughtfully.' Aditi said this as she believed she had a right over Amit. However, she was unaware that a different right was beginning to claim Amit now.

Nikita would always stay close to Amit whenever she came to college. Amit felt a strange emotion, but did not act on it. Nikita was broken-hearted, and she needed Amit's support. He, too, didn't think there was anything wrong in giving her that. They had known each other for a long time and he liked her childlike behaviour. He didn't mind her obstinacy about little things.

Even after a few weeks had passed, Nikita had not recovered from her shock and had agreed to go to Delhi. Initially, she was scared, but agreed when she got to know that Amit would accompany her. Amit was going to Delhi for the first time and Shyam had made all the arrangements. On reaching Delhi, Amit found the atmosphere of Nikita's house strange, putting it down to the behaviour of people who lived in a big city. Nikita belonged to a middle class family of a big city, but seeing their pretentious lifestyle, one could mistake them for a high class family. This is how everyone perceived Nikita in Jabalpur too. He could see Vikram was admired in her family for they asked about him several times, but he did not reply. Nobody was really bothered about Nikita. Amit was surprised when he saw that Nikita's mother had failed to discern her sadness. Her father seemed to be a short-tempered person but Nikita seemed to be closer to him. Whether it was love or fear, it was difficult for Amit to understand.

Amit had seen Delhi for the first time. A big city, high buildings, big cars and wide roads—all this had impressed him in the beginning but he had understood that this world was very different from his own. On Radhika's insistence, he had called her parents too and they had sent a car to pick him up one day. Radhika's family seemed to be rich as they had an old family business. Radhika's parents, her own brother and cousins and several uncles and aunts had met him very cordially. He didn't have to face the cold behaviour he associated with a big city and its lifestyle at Radhika's place as he had at Nikita's. He could understand the difference in Radhika's and Nikita's behaviour much better on seeing their families. When he returned from Radhika's place, Nikita was waiting for him but the others had locked themselves up in their rooms.

The next day, as Amit was preparing to leave in the morning, Nikita came to him and said, 'I will come back with you.'

Amit tried reasoning with her, 'Stay for a few days. You come a little later.'

'No...I don't want to miss my studies.'

She kept insisting and her parents too did not resist much. Her brother anyway didn't seem to have much time to speak to her, but her sister Pranita was quite unhappy about her leaving. However, even though she didn't have a ticket, her obstinacy won.

On their way back, they were supposed to go to Jabalpur via Bhopal as they had not got a direct ticket from the Nizamuddin railway station to Jabalpur. Nikita was entirely dependent on him on both these journeys. At times, she would even fall asleep on his shoulders. Amit could see that she liked his company and the fact that he could help her when she was in this state gave Amit immense happiness. And on their way back, these words of Nikita had forced him to think, 'I am very scared of travelling alone. I would not have been able to reach Jabalpur, if it was not for you...I would have died on the way.' Hearing this, Amit had drifted in the current of her grief.

27

AMIT, Aditi, Shyam and Radhika had passed in the finals but Nikita had not even appeared for the exams. Vikram was not a part of the group any more. Anyway, it didn't really matter to him if he got any supplementaries. All four of them had started their internships. They were given long duties in the hospital ward so that they could gain practical knowledge and Amit could not go home for weeks. Often, Nikita would come to him while he was on duty. She would prepare for her supplementary papers in the duty room itself. Her internship was getting delayed because of the supplementaries.

It was time for Durga Puja and festivities had begun in Jabalpur. Amit was tired of doing his internship duty so he asked Nikita to go with him to see the Durga idols near her hostel and she agreed. Radhika and Shyam had gone to visit Shyam's parents in Narsinghpur for Dussehra. Within a few minutes, Amit sensed that Nikita was not very fond of crowds. She was not very interested in the decorated pandals and the idols.

'Should we go back?' Amit asked seeing her unresponsiveness.

'Whatever you think fit.'

'Come, I will drop you to your hostel.'

'And what about you?'

'I will stay at Shyam's for a while and then go to the hospital. I want to freshen up.'

'It is all right. We'll go to Shyam's flat.'

'Okay.'

Nikita went to the balcony on reaching the flat. Amit made some tea and keeping it on the table with some biscuits, called out to her. She came in and sat down on the ground, placing her head in his lap. Amit stroked her forehead sitting on the chair. There was a sense of belonging in his touch. Amit was an emotional person and he could read into Nikita's loneliness. Her grief made him sad. Like many others, he was attracted to her beauty but now her sad face troubled him. All these years of friendship encouraged him to do something to alleviate her sadness.

Amit had never sat so close to a woman before. Nikita's soft touch and warm breath was making him shiver but he was caressing her forehead, controlling himself. After some time, Nikita looked up at him, her big innocent eyes vacant. Amit averted her gaze because if he would have looked at her for long, he would have cried.

'Do you love me?' Amit could not respond when Nikita asked him this.

'...I need your love.' Saying this, Nikita stood up and embraced him. Amit could hear her heartbeat clearly. He felt its intensity and his judgement got clouded. The circle of her arms was giving him a strange warmth and her body's fragrance encouraged him to move ahead and Amit could not stop himself.

Amit experienced a strange happiness; he could not believe that natural beauty could be experienced like this. Their physical closeness was beyond his expectation. They remained lying down for hours, Nikita still nestling close to him. After making love, Amit had given her the sensation of his being close to her by the touch of her body and Nikita had given him both mental and physical pleasure.

'I will drop you to the hostel,' he said, kissing her forehead.

'No,' Nikita said and held him tightly.

'I have to go to the hospital,' he said softly.

'Go if it is important, but come back soon,' Nikita said kissing his chest.

'Are you going to stay alone here? Won't you be scared?' Amit asked.

'No, your fragrance is with me now,' Nikita said softly, looking into his eyes.

After her appeal, Amit could not leave her and go. Unable to stop himself, they made love again…and this continued all night.

On waking up the next morning, Amit saw Nikita sleeping soundly next to him. He went into the balcony and gazed at the sky. There was a strange freshness in this morning. The slight chill of dawn was tickling him, but as the day progressed, the brightness of the reality began making itself evident. Was this correct? Was he being unfair in the name of help and support? But his heart said, 'No. This was love.' But was he worth Nikita? And what about Vikram? His heart explained again. These are all things of the past; Nikita has forgotten him. But is this good for her? He should speak to Nikita.

He was still struggling with this dilemma when Nikita came and hugged him from behind, 'Don't leave me and go.'

'No, no…' he couldn't say anything beyond this. He did not think it was suitable to ask her the questions that were in his head at that moment. When he came out after a bath, he saw Nikita staring at him.

'I will have to go home in the evening. It has been several days. Ma and Didi must be waiting for me.'

'Okay, when will you meet me next? Tomorrow morning?'

'I will see.'

Amit went to drop Nikita to her hostel on Shyam's scooter in the evening. Today, Nikita sat very close to him, he could feel that she did not want to stay apart from him. She looked at him for long after getting off and said through her eyes, 'Come back soon.'

On reaching home late in the evening, he kept thinking for some time. The battle between his head and heart did not let him sleep. Neither did he get any answers. His head and heart just didn't seem to agree. Nikita's soft touch was weighing on his mind. Malti seemed to sense the change in him and looked at him, slightly bewildered.

The next day when he reached the hospital late in the evening for duty, he saw Nikita walking towards him.

'When did you come?' she asked, her eyes fixed on Amit's face.

'Just now,' Amit said, trying to avoid her gaze.

'Why didn't you come to the hostel to meet me?' There was a note of assertion of rights along with love in her question.

'I was getting late,' Amit said, unable to look into her eyes.

'Come, let's go to the coffee house. I am very hungry,' she held his hand and started pulling him so he could not refuse her. Even at the coffee house, she sat very close to him and did not leave his hand. The coffee house was a busy place but it was even more crowded in the evenings. Although no one was looking at them directly, Amit felt that all eyes were on him.

'Let's go home,' Nikita came closer and whispered into his ear.

'What home?' Amit asked looking at her properly for the first time now.

'Shyam's,' Nikita touched his hands, expressing her desire for him.

'Now? But I am on duty.'

'Tell your friend to look after the work for some time, please,' she said holding his arm tightly.

Nikita's touch had aroused Amit and he found it difficult to control himself. Unable to control the flow of his desires, Amit went with her to Shyam's and soon, Amit was losing himself in Nikita as she embraced him. Both were immersed in the other and their hearts were beating in the same rhythm.

Lovemaking had become their everyday routine. The moment they had satiated their appetite for the morning, they were hungry for the afternoon. The nights were all spent awake and sleep had become a thing of the past. It is impossible to stop a river when it breaks all boundaries and wants to merge with the sea. Thus, they didn't realize how eight days passed.

Radhika had gone to Narsinghpur with Shyam to cement their relationship but in Jabalpur, Amit and Nikita had already become tied up in a bond. Staying at Shyam's place, Nikita and Amit would cook and eat and then get immersed in love. The body's thirst was stronger than the stomach's hunger. Amit would manage to go to the hospital sometimes with a lot of difficulty. Nikita would not let him go anywhere else.

By the time Radhika returned, Nikita had changed. She looked really happy. Even Shyam had noticed a transformation in Amit. On being asked, both of them said that they had had a lot of fun during the Durga Puja. Once Shyam was back, Amit and Nikita had lost the place for their rendezvous. After his hospital duty, Amit would take Nikita to the temple in the colony and on a few occasions, to 'Pisanhari ki madhiya,' perched on the small hillock in front of the college. Pisanhari ki madhiya is a place of worship for Jains in Jabalpur. It is said that an elderly woman had got this temple made by grinding foodgrain. Since it is a small hillock, one has to climb a few stairs to reach there, but the view from the top is panoramic.

Nikita would almost always hold his hands while walking. She did not have any hesitation, but Amit wanted to stay slightly far because he was both afraid and shy. He wanted to hide from scrutinizing eyes. Even when he had to spend two nights in the hospita, Nikita visited him there. Amit asked her to return to the hostel but she did not want to.

One night, around 11 p.m., Amit was at home. He had not been able to meet Nikita that day. He was resting after dinner when he heard a voice calling out his name. Amit woke up, confused, and when he opened the door he saw Nikita, standing with Shyam.

'What happened?'

'She insisted that she wanted to meet you. I tried explaining but she would just not listen. Anyway, I need to leave. Radhika is alone at the flat.' Shyam prepared to leave saying this.

'And how will you go back?' Amit was utterly confused seeing Nikita standing there. How could he call her inside in front of Ma?

'I will leave in some time. I just wanted to meet you,' Nikita said, averting her eyes.

Malti had come to the door by then and on hearing Nikita, she said, 'How will you go without any refreshment? Have some tea and go. You have come to our place for the first time, come inside.'

Shyam was in a hurry. He said, 'Amit, Radhika is alone at home. She had come with Nikita from the hostel. I will have to leave. Aunty, I will come some other time. Anyway, I visit often.'

'All right, you go, beta. Anyhow, it's not safe for a girl to go back this late. Beti, I hope you are not in a hurry. Leave tomorrow morning,' Ma said, clasping Nikita by the shoulder and taking her inside the house.

Nikita was amazed at Malti's welcome and there was happiness on her face. Shyam was smiling seeing her go inside, but Amit was still confused. Supriya greeted her too, with her happy 'Aa, aa.' That night Nikita stayed up talking to Ma for a long time and slept beside her. Amit could hear her sweet, loving voice in the next room till late at night.

Section 4

28

'RADHIKA? This is Aditi.'

'Aditi? How come you are here?' Radhika expressed her surprise.

'Hold on, hold on, don't ask so many questions at the same time. I am calling you because Amit asked me to. Don't give him a call.' Aditi was direct.

'Why? What happened?' Radhika asked expressing her fear and surprise.

'Last night he suffered a heart attack. When he regained consciousness, he asked me to call you.' Aditi breathed heavily. There was sadness in her voice.

'What!' Radhika screamed on the phone.

'He is fine now but is still under observation.'

'Poor Amit!' Radhika heaved a sigh of relief.

'Radhika, what is this all about? I cannot understand what's troubling him.'

'Amit is just very unlucky. Let's just leave it at that.'

'How? And Nikita?'

'What about her? Haven't you met her recently?'

'No. I visited them once when I got the Jabalpur posting. She did not even come out of her room—what could I have done? Even Amit talks very rarely these days. He didn't even invite me to his place again, neither did he visit us. Yes, people do say that Nikita is depressed.'

'No, no, she's schizophrenic.'

'What! Since when? She seemed to be fine in college.'

'A disturbed mind behind a beautiful face—completely disorganized. She was my roommate in college and I used to feel that she was just stubborn and spoilt. At times, she would not sleep for nights and would fight about little things. You remember how she once fought so badly with me over the issue of cleaning the room? She didn't do anything on her own, but would shout at the drop of a hat. But now I understand that that was the beginning of depression. Actually, these were the symptoms of bipolar depression. But no one knows when it became schizophrenia. Anyway, I believe a trigger can set it off, otherwise it stays submerged. Her condition was quite bad some time back. I guess she is better now.'

'But how do you know all this?'

'She is being treated in Delhi by a psychiatrist, Dr Verma. We know him so he told me a little of what was going on.'

'And Nikita's parents were also in Delhi, right? And so are her siblings. Don't they do anything?'

'Forget about help, I think they just aggravate her sickness.'

'But how?' a surprised Aditi asked.

'Do you remember Sood Uncle? Nikita's father? Such an aggressive person! When he came to our college, he picked fights with people. Like Nikita, he also has mood swings and suffers from depression. Thankfully, her mother is sensible and takes good care of him. But, she did not look after her children well. The others have been okay but since Nikita was the younger one, she was spoilt and always had to have her own way. She is full of anger, especially at her parents, and she takes it out on Amit and the children.'

'Didn't her siblings try to explain things to her?'

'Her twin sister is sensible. One day, she told me that Nikita is stupid enough to listen to their mother, who can be very interfering. After she got married, she had told her mother she didn't want any advice from her—that's why she stays happy. As far as the brother is concerned, he is henpecked. So only Nikita remains for the parents to boss over. They don't even realize that what they say affects Nikita negatively,' Radhika explained.

'How do they behave with Amit?'

'They don't talk to him politely and insult him every now and then. Initially, Amit would put up with it but now he doesn't visit them and has stopped talking to them. But these people still instigate Nikita and drive her crazy.' There was anger in Radhika's voice.

'But they are educated people! Why are they spoiling their daughter's life?' Aditi was confused.

'Perhaps they are just ignorant. Who knows?' Then Radhika changed the topic. She asked, 'When did you return to India? Amit told me that you haven't got married yet…'

'It was wonderful living in London but one misses one's country. Ma was missing it too, so we returned. As far as marriage is concerned, I was too busy studying and by the time I started thinking about marriage, I thought I was way past the marriageable age. I never fell in love or met the right person. But let's forget about all this. You have to tell me what Amit is worried about and why he asked me to call you?'

Aditi was lying down on her bed with her eyes closed. One hand was under her head and she held the cordless phone with the other.

'I don't know much about it but Amit is trying to send his daughter away from home. He wants to put her in a hostel. He is very worried about her and wants her to stay away from the atmosphere in the house.'

'I see,' Aditi said pensively, but she wasn't really satisfied with Radhika's reply. She asked, 'How is Shyam? You both turned out to be secretive musketeers. You didn't let anyone get to know about your relationship in college…how many children do you have?' Aditi closed her eyes and her college days zoomed in her mind.

'Just one son.'

They chatted a little and then hung up. Aditi went into deep thought, saddened by Nikita's plight—she was so beautiful, yet mentally so disturbed. On the other hand, there was Amit, who had suffered such misfortune in his life.

Her thoughts turned to her own life and the bleakness of it. There was no one to live for, no relationship that could be an anchor. She had studied very hard in college and was rewarded by her uncle, who had left a huge bank balance for her, specifying in his will that she was to use it to study abroad. After completing her postgraduate studies in London, she had started working in the same college, but had to return at her mother's insistence. She did not want to go into private practice in India and like Amit, she took the Union Public Service Commission examination and got into the Indian Railways as a doctor. Her mother had grown old now, and wasn't keeping well, but she had tried very hard to get Aditi married, but Aditi was too busy to cooperate. She knew she was not bad-looking, but somehow no one had approached her… and Amit had remained only a friend.

Aditi thought of how ill Amit had looked in the hospital and the worried expression of Dr Khurana, who had examined him. He and the chief medical superintendent, Dr Sharma, had discussed his high ECG graph and the change in the T-wave graph that indicated the intensity of the attack. Amit had suffered the attack because blood had not been able to reach the arteries. He would have to be careful going forward. That is why…

'No alcohol, no smoking and no stress,' the chief had said softly.

Then Dr Sharma had asked Akanksha, 'How is your mother, beta?'

'She is fine,' Akanksha had replied, lowering her eyes.

'Don't worry, everything will be fine. Aditi, I met one of your patients at a party the other day and she praised you for your efficiency. You are good at cosmetic surgery. There are no marks on her stomach! I told her you are talented, so keep it up!'

Aditi felt that at least her profession gave her a purpose in life, even though it did not really fill the void deep within her. Even Amit, her childhood friend, had not confided in her about Nikita and this hurt her. Amit had never invited her home and she had assumed the reason was that Nikita didn't like his friendship with her. She wondered why she could not get close to anybody.

In the morning, after spending the night in the hospital, Aditi had gone to Amit's house to pick up her car. When Aniruddh came out of his room, she saw that his eyes were swollen. It seemed that he had not slept all night. He asked about his father and she told him that he was conscious and being given the best treatment. Then she asked him about Nikita, but he did not reply—in fact, she read anger on his face at her question.

She spoke soothingly, 'You should visit your father when your sister comes back today. She'll call you up if she needs anything. There is no need to worry. Now, I am going back home to rest.'

'Thank you, Aunty,' is all Aniruddh said, as she sat in her car and switched the engine on.

She felt sorry for Akanksha and Aniruddh. Maybe, Amit was right in wanting to send Akanksha away. As she thought she would speak to him in the evening, Aditi fell asleep.

29

'HELLO, has Mom woken up?' Akanksha called Aniruddh at home.

'No. Forget about her. How is Papa?' There was worry in Aniruddh's voice

Akanksha said tearfully, 'He is fine now, but it seems that he won't ever recover completely. God knows what will happen…why does Papa have to sufffer?'

'If he keeps listening to what Mom says, this is what will happen. How many times have I told him that if he treats Mom like delicate porcelain, her condition will only worsen and create problems for himself too. But, when does he ever listen? What a bloody life we have!' Aniruddh's voice was full of anger and pain.

'Look, Ani, you will not fight with Mom when she gets up today. Why don't you understand? Have you eaten anything? Did Lakshmi Didi come?'

'Yes, she has.'

'Get her to make some tea; there are biscuits too. Have them and when Mom gets up, give her tea and biscuits too. She needs to line her stomach because of those strong medicines. I will come in some time and cook. Do you have to go to school?'

'What can I say? I need to go, but in such circumstances how will I? I'll come to pick you up on the scooter, okay?'

'Okay, where is Lakshmi? I will tell her to make tea for you.'

'I will tell her,' Aniruddh said loudly.

'Okay, fine. Why are you screaming?' Akanksha said softly and hung up.

Akanksha and Aniruddh were close but their temperaments were different—while Akanksha was quiet, serious and loving, Aniruddh was short-tempered. Akanksha did not do too well in her studies as she had to take on the responsibility of running the house at a very young age. She was very attached to her father and took very good care of her mother, even though Nikita would keep yelling at her. Despite her mother's behaviour, Akanksha would cry for her mother, aware of her illness. She had a special love for her brother. Aniruddh always achieved good results in school. His relationship with his mother was loving, but he would fight with her if she shouted at Akki Didi. Akanksha was a little scared of Aniruddh, but she mothered him and looked after him.

The railway bungalows had servant's quarters or outhouses attached to them. Lakshmi bai stayed in the outhouse attached to Dr Amit Saxena's bungalow and helped Akanksha with the cooking and cleaning. Her husband was a fruit-seller and her children were young. She was a simple, sensitive person. On hearing about Amit, she expressed her concern, cleaned the house, made tea and left. Aniruddh knocked again at his mother's door, but she did not get up. Seeing her sleeping from the window, his anger turned to rage, when suddenly the phone rang... Thinking that it would be Akanksha, he ran to answer it, but it was his friend, 'You aren't coming to school today?'

'No, I am not feeling very well. I have fever. I will call you later.' He did not like talking about the situation at home with others so he hung up quickly.

Worrying about his father, he decided to go to the hospital. He jumped on his scooter, revved the engine and sped there. When he reached the hospital he rushed into his father's room but then stopped short, shocked. There was his father, pale and gaunt, with an oxygen mask on his face. Choking back his tears, he leaned forward and stroked his father's forehead.

Tears welled up in Amit's eyes when he saw his son, but he swallowed them.

His first words were, 'Is your mother all right? Take care of her.'

'Stop worrying about her and take care of yourself,' Aniruddh said angrily.

Akanksha said softly to her father, 'I will come back soon after doing some household work. I'll wake up Mom too,' she said. Amit nodded, trying to smile. Then she returned home with Aniruddh.

Nikita had still not woken up. She usually got up much after the children had gone to school, so they didn't see her till they came back home. On this day, when she stirred and opened her eyes, it was late afternoon.

Aniruddh could not contain himself and blurted out, 'You are sleeping and Papa has had a heart attack. He is in the hospital now.'

Nikita's face was swollen and she looked weak. Bewilderment and then concern flitted across her face. Akanksha brought in the tea.

'Mom, have some tea.'

Nikita's expression changed and she looked at her daughter with disdain, saying bitingly, 'Will you kill me too? See what has happened because of you? Generally, you pretend to be your father's favourite—what happened now?'

'Mom, don't say anything to Didi,' Aniruddh growled.

'Oh! So now you have managed to take your brother to your side too. You're all out to ruin me with everyone's support.'

Akanksha did not say a word and went out of the room, pulling Aniruddh along with her.

Nikita stumbled as she groggily got out of bed. She splashed her face with water in the bathroom and wet her hair with her hands. Then she went straight to her phone to call her mother. She said, crying, 'Ma, Amit has suffered a heart attack. He is in the hospital,'

'Is he fine now?' the voice was loud from the other side.

'Yes, I have heard he is fine.'

'I have told him so many times not to drink, but he just doesn't listen. This had to happen one day. If anything untoward happens, what will happen to you, beta?...We are very worried about you. How are you? Take care of yourself.'

Nikita was crying like a little girl.

'See, your father doesn't keep very well and your brother has too much work. Let me see if your brother will agree and I'll send him over…if you don't like it there, come here for some time. Don't worry. What can we do? Amit doesn't even talk to us. Anyway, God will see us through and don't tell your father otherwise, he will get worried. Okay, take care.' And she hung up the phone.

Aniruddh was listening to the conversation on the parallel line in another room. He was furious and told his sister, 'These people don't feel any shame. Here our father is at death's door and they are saying that it has happened because of alcohol. Has anyone ever thought why he drinks? They won't do anything for him but will keep criticizing him. What can we do? It's our mother's weakness that she hasn't understood them till now. She pretends to be sick here but is absolutely fine when she goes there. Why doesn't she show them her real face? There she behaves very nicely knowing that she can't get away with bad behaviour. They are selfish and cunning people, unlike Papa.'

'You shouldn't talk like this. They are our grandparents,' Akanksha said, trying to calm Aniruddh.

'What grandparents? I have observed them ever since I was a child, and I've seen how they kept instigating Mom against Papa,' Aniruddh said loudly.

Both of them did not see that their mother had come into the room. They turned only when they heard her raised voice, 'Look, don't say anything about my parents.'

'Then tell them to not say anything about my father too,' Aniruddh shouted.

'This is all this girl's doing. All day she keeps instigating everyone against me and my family,' Nikita said staring hard at Akanksha.

Akanksha pleaded with her mother with folded hands, asking her not to blame her. Aniruddh shouted, 'Look, Mom, don't say anything to Didi, otherwise…'

'Otherwise what? You will hit me?'

And then Nikita started hitting herself on the head with her slippers. Akanksha tried to stop her but she pushed her and went inside, slamming the door behind her. The sound of her hitting herself could be heard from the room for some time.

Akanksha was scared and ran to the door, knocking hard and crying. When Nikita did not open it, she ran out and peeped in from the window in the garden and saw that her mother was blabbering, pulling her own hair and sitting on the bed, twisted up.

Akanksha said softly through the window, 'Mom, I am saying sorry. Ani is a little short-tempered but he loves you. Please open the door and say whatever you have to—to me.'

'Tell him not to say anything about my parents,' Nikita said, remaining on her bed.

'Okay, I will tell him, he won't say anything. He is a child, he doesn't understand,' Sobbing loudly, Akanksha went back into the bungalow. She stood at the door for a long time, banging the door to her mother's room. She explained to Aniruddh, 'You should not talk like this.'

By now, Aniruddh's anger had vanished, horrified as he was by his mother's reaction. He was scared that his mother might do something untoward. Even Papa was in the hospital...and he had started crying. He was wiping his tears constantly but they just refused to stop and words flowed with his tears. 'We are nothing to her—what kind of disease is this?' he sobbed.

Akanksha tried calming Aniruddh down and said, 'Don't worry, everything will be fine.'

Once he had controlled himself, she sent him to bathe and went in to cook. In the meantime, she called her friend to tell her that she wouldn't be able to attend classes even today. When she had finished cooking, she managed to get Nikita to open the door and said softly, 'Mom, please take a bath and eat something, you must be hungry. I have to go to the hospital now.'

Nikita got up and went to the bathroom without looking at Akanksha. Quietly, Akanksha kept her food on the bedside table filled the jug with water, thinking her mother would feel thirsty after having her medicines. And then closing the door behind her, she went to her own room to get ready. Since she was getting late for the hospital, she requested Aniruddh to drop her on the scooter. He was silent, but she kept explaining to him, 'Don't say anything to Mom. Hasn't Papa told you several times that she is not stable mentally? She will get better if we give her love. She is our mother and we should try to understand her…now don't start her off again.'

Aniruddh nodded. When he dropped her off, Akanksha said, 'Don't think too much and take care of yourself.'

Akanksha saw that the lift had already gone up. Not wanting to wait for it, she ran up the stairs. When she reached the second floor, she saw that the afternoon round of the doctors was over. A group of doctor and nurses was standing there, waiting. She knew each one of them. When she reached the room, she saw her father lying on the bed. His eyes were fixed on the door and it seemed that he had been waiting for her. As soon as he saw her, he asked anxiously, 'How is your mother?'

'She is fine. She was asking about you and was worried,' Akanksha said caressing her father's head.

Amit smiled when he heard that. He knew it was a lie, but knew his daughter was trying to protect him.

Meanwhile, Akanksha busied herself giving her father his medicines and making him eat the watery dal that was on his table, following the nurse's instructions carefully.

In the evening, Aditi came in, accompanied by Sunita. Akanksha could not recognize her at first because she looked frail and old.

Aditi asked Akanksha, 'How is she?' and then looking at Amit said, 'And how are you?'

Amit nodded silently. Sunita stroked Akanksha's face and then said to Amit, 'Son, what is all this? I have been very worried since I heard you'd fallen sick. I came because I could not bear it. Anyway, don't worry, everything will be fine. God is there to look after us.

You don't come to meet us, so I keep asking Aditi about you. This time if you don't come and visit after being discharged from the hospital, I will not spare you,' and she again turned to Akanksha and patted her head lovingly.

'She is just like her aunt. She looks like Supriya, she is very sweet…' she had tears in her eyes while saying this. Amit turned to the other side and closed his eyes.

Aditi looked at the mother angrily and signalled to her to be quiet. There was absolute silence in the room. After some time, Aditi said, 'I will drop Ma off and come back. Please let me know if you need anything, and Amit, I have already spoken to Radhika. Don't worry, everything is fine.'

Sunita's words were reverberating in Amit's ears. He looked at Akanksha keenly after they had left…she was right, she did look like Supriya. He experienced a strange pain in his heart as he remembered his sister. When he closed his eyes and tried forgetting her, Supriya's face appeared in a blur.

30

EMOTIONS can be expressed in many ways. The only problem is how much of it is understood by the person it is directed at. It depends on whether one is able to read the other's emotions. Even more important is the strength of the bond with the person. A bond of love since childhood ensures an understanding of the loved one's state of mind without any words being spoken. For example, a mother understands most of what her child feels without the child saying anything. In the same way, a father can read his child's thoughts easily? Children, too, begin to understand their parents, brothers understand their sisters and vice versa. It is because they share a bond of love.

But sometimes a person you love a lot might not love you back.

Since childhood, Supriya could neither speak nor walk and her limbs couldn't function properly. It was polio, said the doctors of the government hospital and it could not be treated. Another doctor had said that it was cerebral palsy, which is why her body had not been able to develop according to her age. Masterji and Malti's means were limited and therefore, they had accepted her plight as God-given.

In his childhood, Amit had seen how his mother looked after her daughter. She had limitless love in her heart for her and Supriya too had never felt that she was a burden.

In their home, all of them understood her emotions and whatever she wanted to say. Amit would meet her as soon as he came back from school and would stay up with her all night if she needed attention. She lay on her bed peacefully and the spark in her eyes when she heard their voices was heartwarming. Once they were home, they would sit around her. She would listen to everything carefully and talk to them through her eyes. Amit had never seen hopelessness in her eyes. Even when they had lost their father as children, she was sad but not distraught.

She had been with her mother through all her hardship and troubles. Earlier, whenever she called out, her mother would be there in an instant, but later, when Malti had to go to the school to work, she was alone for long stretches of the day. Gita and Sunita, and at times even Kamla, would check on her when she called out and even otherwise, visit her at regular intervals. But when she could not control her body, she would end up soiling the bed. When Malti returned, Supriya would be ashamed of what had happened, but Malti would clean everything up and change her clothes, talking soothingly to her as if she was a small child, 'My little baby, so you have dirtied yourself again? It is all right. It doesn't matter.'

There was so much love in these words that Surpriya would soon be smiling. Amit would help his mother on the days he returned home early. Both Amit and Malti, after returning from school, would sit with Supriya and narrate the day's incidents to her. She was the happiest when Amit got admitted to the medical college. She had always dreamt that Amit would grow up to become a doctor and would treat her.

As Amit's studies became tougher, he started coming home late. Firstly, the college was far off and he would stay back to study in the library. But even then, Supriya would not sleep till he returned from college.

Aditi, too, would meet Supriya almost every day while she was in the neighbourhood and could communicate with her well.

Amit got busier with each passing year. First college, and then the institute. But he would rush to meet Supriya the moment he came home. He could not come back home for weeks during his internship and missed Supriya even in the hospital. Then he and Nikita had fallen in love and at that time he had not come back home even once in those ten days. Even when he returned, he would look tired and worried, and did not share his secret with his sister. She seemed to understand and when Nikita came to their place late that night, Supriya looked very happy, smiling sweetly. Nikita had not spoken much to her, but Supriya seemed to be attracted by her beauty. Her smile had said a lot to Amit.

Once Radhika and Shyam were back, Amit and Nikita could not meet at Shyam's place. They went to the temple in the evening and had breakfast at the coffee house together in the morning, but did not have a place where they could make love. When Nikita began her internship, they saw to it that they were given their duty at the same time.

When Amit's professors enquired about his future plans, he said very simply, 'I will stay in India, in Jabalpur itself. First of all, I don't have the money to study abroad and even if I get a scholarship, it is not possible for me to leave my mother and sick sister behind. I will pursue my studies here, I don't need to go anywhere for that. Why should I leave home for that? My family means everything to me, so why should I leave them?'

The dean was very surprised. Amit was a very bright boy and he could get an admission wherever he liked. But such love for one's family was rare in today's world.

One day, Amit was on duty in the casualty ward and Nikita was in the general labour ward. Late in the evening, she came to Amit, looking worried, 'Amit, I need to talk to you about something important. Let's go to the coffee house.'

'What happened?'

'Come along, I will tell you there,' she said, pulling him away.

When they reached the coffee house, she looked into his eyes, held his hands and said, 'Tell me you won't leave me.'

'You know I won't—but what is the matter?'

'We will have to get married soon. I am pregnant,' she said shyly.

'What?' Amit experienced a strange joy. But several niggling questions crowded his mind. His family would not object, but what about Nikita's parents? Would they agree?

'Have you spoken to your family?'

'That is what I wanted to talk to you about...how should we go about it?'

'What if they don't agree, considering my circumstances?'

'This is what we need to figure out...how to convince them... we will have to do something.'

'You have to be open and frank with them.'

'Yes, yes,' Nikita said, her face bright with joy but Amit suddenly felt surrounded by a million responsibilities.

Amit could not sleep that night...he kept thinking and worrying about the future. Was marriage the right thing to do considering he was still doing his internship? Would Nikita be able to adjust to life with Ma and Supriya at home? What would Nikita's parents say?

'No, no, Nikita will love Ma and Supriya because they are such simple people. A beautiful daughter-in-law like Nikita, who is also a doctor...what more would anybody want? But what about Nikita's parents? They won't agree...they seem to be quite arrogant. Will they go against their daughter's wish? And in her condition! Well, they could get the child aborted...but will Nikita let that happen? No, no...'

Amit was staring at the wall in front of him—as the rays of the morning sun were already lighting it and he hadn't slept a wink. He would become a doctor soon, he thought. They didn't have any money now, but that would change soon. He knew he should first talk to Ma and Supriya about it.

Early in the morning, Amit went to Supriya and stroked her forehead. Supriya's eyes shone with happiness. For the last few days, she had been worried about Amit. She understood and felt everything...what was it that had been troubling her brother? She would ask him but not today. Thinking this, she smiled at him. Amit again caressed Supriya's cheeks and called out to his mother lovingly.

Malti came out of the kitchen and was very happy to see both brother and sister together after such a long time. She was silently thanking God when Amit's question caught her by surprise, 'Ma, do you like Nikita?'

'Why? What is the matter?'

'Ma, we want to get married to each other.'

Malti could not believe her ears. She could see various emotions on her son's face and felt overjoyed. She had seen Nikita that night, and thought she was very pretty. Malti had understood that there was something between them that night itself but had remained quiet, smiling inwardly. Supriya expressed her happiness by making loud noises. She looked at her brother and spoke to him through her eyes, 'She is very beautiful. I like her.' Amit understood that and hugged his sister, but sadly, Supriya could not lift her arms to hug her brother yet again.

31

AFTER some time, Amit told Malti about Nikita's pregnancy too. Initially, she was a little shocked but then she thought, 'They are both educated, and are getting married, so there's nothing wrong about it though they could have waited.' She bowed in front of the gods ensconced in a small niche in the kitchen in gratitude. She touched her son's forehead with love and assured him of her full support.

Amit went to the hostel and met Nikita. He held her hands and said excitedly, 'My mother is very happy that we're getting married! We have her blessings.'

She smiled, but Amit's mother's acceptance meant nothing to Nikita. It's a human trait not to value something that comes to us easily. On the other hand, Amit was extremely happy. He said, 'Ma has asked you to come home.'

'Okay.'

'We should tell Shyam, Radhika and Aditi too,' Amit said with a sense of belonging. He believed that a couple should discuss matters and take each other's advice before any decisions.

Nikita was not smiling any more and replied coldly, 'All right.'

Amit saw the change in her expression and asked, concerned, 'What happened? Are you feeling unwell?'

But Nikita did not answer.

Amit saw that the enthusiasm with which Nikita had told him about the pregnancy yesterday was gone. He thought that perhaps she was uncertain about marriage. Maybe, she was scared of her parents! And he touched Nikita's cheeks with love, trying to reassure her.

'You get ready and reach the coffee house, I will bring Shyam and Radhika.'

He found Shyam and Radhika in the same ward and when he told them the news, they were delighted.

Shyam embraced him and said, patting his back, 'You turned out to be a real hero, my friend. One who sticks by his word and principles.'

Radhika loved her friend and there were tears of happiness in her eyes. She smiled and congratulated him.

Amit didn't have the courage to talk to Aditi. Where would he begin? He had become quite distant from her ever since he had got involved with Nikita. Amit had hidden details about his relationship with Nikita from her but even then he had a soft spot for Aditi. They had been friends since childhood but he was slightly shy and scared of her. He requested Radhika to tell her instead. Initially, Radhika found that strange but agreed. Radhika went to Aditi's ward and told her that Amit had decided to marry Nikita.

Aditi couldn't believe her ears. She said, 'It is good that Amit loves Nikita, but does Nikita love him as much?' Aditi was very mature for her age and this question was a pertinent one.

'Yes, yes, why not?' Radhika said innocently.

'Great, so where is Mr Bridegroom? Come, let's meet him,' and both of them walked towards the coffee house.

Aditi met Amit with great enthusiasm, 'So, this is why my friend wasn't available for me!'

Amit smiled.

'And where is the bride?' Aditi joked.

'She is coming—she's in the hostel.'

'So, sir knows exactly where she is!' Aditi said jovially and all of them laughed. When Nikita reached there after some time, both Aditi and Radhika hugged her. Radhika started crying with happiness. But Nikita's smile was forced.

'Not this unhappy expression, we want to see the original Nikita,' Shyam said teasing her.

'Maybe she is worried about what her parents will say and she is not feeling very well,' Radhika explained.

'Arre yaar, what is the problem? Amit is a doctor, a topper. He is smart, good-looking, doesn't have any weaknesses—what else would the parents of a girl want?' Aditi said.

'That is true, Nikita. You should talk to your parents and get the date fixed. We will have to make all the arrangements and we don't have much time.' Shyam said, trying to show Amit and Nikita that he would shoulder responsibilities like a good friend.

Suddenly, Nikita's bad mood seemed to vanish and she began to laugh. It seemed as if she had emerged from a void. All of them were befuddled for a moment but then joined in with her laughter. Shyam found this sudden change strange, but thought... maybe she was upset about her parents and felt better after hearing Aditi's words.

Shyam took Nikita to the STD booth to speak to her parents and all of them went along. Hesitantly, Nikita dialled the number. When her mother picked up the phone, Nikita wasted no time with any preamble and blurted out, 'Ma, I have decided to get married!'

There was a question from the other side. 'No, no, not him. The one who had come with me the last time—Amit. Ma, please tell Papa and Bhaiya. I am in a hurry. Please come here soon then we can go ahead with our plans.' After listening to her mother for some time, she said, 'No, I cannot wait any longer. The circumstances are such. They are not in a hurry, I am. Why don't you understand?' It seemed that there was a barrage of questions as Nikita was answering continuously, 'Yes, just his mother. She stays with him... that is not a problem. He is nice, simple and truthful, looks after me and is very bright. I will tell you the date, you people just come.'

Amit was listening to all this quietly. Nikita was as loud and chirpy now as she had been quiet earlier.

Once her conversation was done, Shyam got down to business, 'Okay, all of us are going to Amit's place in the evening. We will have to adjust our duties in the ward and I also have to go to the advocate and get a date for the marriage. Three of you go to

Amit's place and make arrangements. We will come soon.' Shyam asked Amit to rush.

Aditi took Radhika and Nikita to her place and told her mother about Amit and Nikita. Sunita could not believe it for a minute, her emotions were visible on her face...happiness that Aditi's friends were getting married and worry for her daughter—would she ever get married? And what was in her mind came to her lips, 'Please make her understand too...'

Aditi looked at her mother and said, 'I want to study further, I have to do a lot of things. I don't want to get tied down.'

To everyone's dismay and surprise, Nikita got extremely upset on hearing this and began sobbing. Aditi and Radhika could not understand why as Aditi had merely voiced a gentle protest. When she did not stop crying even after Aditi tried to calm her down, Radhika called Shyam at the flat, worried. She told him to send Amit to Aditi's house immediately. When Amit came, he tried to pacify Nikita but it took a long time. Aditi felt very guilty and was relieved only when Nikita quietened down.

Seeing all of them agitated, Sunita tried to lighten the atmosphere by saying, 'Come children, I will make something sweet for you. Relax now.'

In the evening, the friends gathered in Amit's house. This was a rare occasion for Amit's family. Malti was excited, pleased to see her future daughter-in-law. She had taken out her wedding necklace to give her.

Malti offered the necklace to Nikita saying, 'It is the custom in our house to give something as a token of love to the daughter-in-law when she comes home for the first time after marriage. Since you have come today, I am giving it to you now instead of waiting. I hope you like it.'

'She likes Amit, Aunty—the necklace is a token of your love and love is priceless. What do you say, Nikita?' Aditi said.

'Yes, look at my necklace, Aunty. It is thick and old-fashioned. Shyam's mother gave this to me when I visited her the first time.

I don't ever take it off,' Radhika said innocently.

Hearing this, Shyam laughed.

'Okay, now touch your mother-in-law's feet and take her blessings,' Sunita commanded.

Nikita did as she was told. Suddenly, Supriya called out and they turned to look at her. She was smiling and looking at Nikita with expectation in her eyes.

Aditi held Nikita by the hand and took her to Supriya, 'This is Amit's sister, friend, guide...everything.'

Nikita didn't say anything. Later, Radhika went in to help Malti and Sunita in the kitchen and Aditi sat next to Supriya, talking to her. Nikita sat on a chair quietly. Amit and Shyam were sitting outside, making plans.

After dinner, Nikita wanted to stay back with Amit but Malti said, 'Beta, after the marriage you can stay here. Tonight you must go back to your hostel, okay?'

She asked Amit to drop Nikita to the hostel and all of them said goodbye. Sunita hugged Malti on leaving and there were tears in both their eyes....

Supriya was happy, but something was troubling her—Nikita had not hugged her or talked to her. Maybe she was shy or maybe, she didn't talk much anyway. She couldn't stop herself from feeling anxious and a crease of worry appeared on her brow.

32

THE date for the court marriage had been decided. Nikita's parents had arrived that morning. Even after a lot of insistence on Shyam's part, they had refused to stay at his flat, opting for a hotel, instead. They were supposed to have the pheras after the court marriage in the day followed by dinner at the hotel at night. All their friends from college, school friends and neighbours had congregated.

Amit wanted to take Supriya along in the evening but could not figure out how to. They had all bought new clothes for the occasion and he got a new dress for his sister too. Malti had put it on Supriya in the morning and Amit teased on seeing her, 'You are looking very beautiful...just like a heroine.'

Supriya was embarrassed, then she was delighted when she saw her brother in his brand-new suit. In the evening, all of them went away, leaving her alone. She felt angry at God and unhappy for the first time. Her eyes were fixed on the door and as the night darkened, her loneliness deepened. She could barely wait for everyone to come home.

Then, at last, she could hear the sound of excited voices. Nikita came in, wearing a beautiful red sari. late at night, with Malti and Amit close behind her. There was a new gaiety in the house and all the neighbours trooped in, exclaiming at how pretty Nikita looked. Supriya was still lying alone in a corner...what else could she do?

She thought, 'I should be reasonable. Amit's new wife has come home and she should be welcomed properly.' She knew she should make an effort to smile and welcome the newcomer, but she was unable to do so.

She lay there staring at the backs of the people in the crowd and when her grief crossed all boundaries, tears flowed from her eyes. The agony made her wet the bed but today she didn't call out for anyone.

When the guests had left, Malti came to her and seeing her clothes soiled said, like she always did, 'My messy baby.' But Supriya didn't smile, her sadness overwhelming.

Amit sat next to Supriya and was talking to her like he used to every day, when suddenly Nikita came in and stroked his head. She said naughtily, 'Will you spend the night talking to your sister? When will you talk to me? It is the night of our love.' Then she pulled him up to take him to his room. She hadn't even looked at Supriya.

Amit couldn't help feeling that she should have sat next to Supriya and talked to her a little. Their lovemaking could have waited for a while.

At night, after they had made love, Amit's mind wandered... does a woman desire to break all existing ties that a man has when she binds herself to him? She had come to me, in my arms, shouldn't she too accept me as I was? She is a woman and a doctor, so how had she failed to understand the psychology of a handicapped person? Maybe she was thinking only like a woman and did not want to share him with anyone else...but couldn't she have waited for a little while? He had seen love and affection for Nikita in Supriya's eyes but she remained waiting...Nikita had not given even a second to Supriya.

Amit's silence troubled Nikita. She took him in her arms and said, 'I don't like being away from you even for a minute.' Amit melted in Nikita's love once again, forgetting Supriya for the time being.

The rooms in the house were one behind another and the kitchen was attached to the room at the back. Beyond that was the bathroom. Anyone who had to use the bathroom would have to cross the room at the back. Malti wanted to go to the bathroom but stopped after seeing her son and daughter-in-law. She decided that she would give the room at the front to Amit and Nikita, whereas Supriya and Malti would take the room at the back.

Amit woke up early. Nikita was still sleeping. Malti was working noiselessly in the kitchen as she didn't want to disturb her daughter-in-law. She had just come to the house, was from a rich family... Malti was thinking about the difference in her own and Nikita's background.

Nikita called out for Amit as soon as she woke up. He was reading the paper sitting next to Supriya.

'Good morning.'

She yelled, 'Come here.'

When Amit went to her, she was smiling. Malti was working in the kitchen but Nikita barely paid any attention to her. Amit remained quiet and sat next to Nikita but he was wondering...of course, it was only the first day, but it would have been so nice if Nikita would have helped mother in the kitchen...forget about help, she hadn't even spoken to Supriya and Ma yet...maybe, Nikita was expecting other things. Normally, couples went for a honeymoon after their marriage. They had not been able to go away and then the house was very small...but couldn't she wait? He would buy a new house as soon as he had some money...all these thoughts jumbled up in Amit's head. After all, he was a sensitive person and was always trying to weigh situations. But he could not get all his answers...he remained sitting next to Nikita and reading the paper.

Days passed in this manner. He had noticed that at times Nikita went very quiet and at others she would talk a lot with Ma. She would smile and ask how Supriya was once in a while but never sat next to her and talked to her. Amit tried to understand the reason behind this but could not figure it out.

33

WEAK and disabled, Supriya was very strong mentally. Her hearing and understanding were acute and she had understood that her sister-in-law did not like her much. She had begun feeling like a burden now. It had been only a few days since the marriage and Amit had already seen sadness and detachment in his sister's eyes.

Supriya understood her mother better than she understood herself. Now she was completely dependent on her. Earlier, Amit would help her in a few day-to-day things but now, after his marriage, he was unable to do so. Nikita would get very angry if he met Supriya first after coming back home and would create a huge fuss about it, as if she had been wronged. Malti would send Amit off to her thinking that she needed her husband's love; and it was possible that she craved Amit's love more because of her pregnancy. Malti tried to explain the situation to Supriya, to make her understand that her brother had another person in his life. Supriya began to accept the fact that her mother was her only support now.

A bond with another person is delicate like a flower, but it can also be confining. There are ties that we accept from the heart with happiness and there are ties that we are forced to accept against our wishes.

Amit and Supriya shared the special bond that exists between a brother and a sister. Amit showered Supriya with love and she asserted her right over him. Supriya liked the fact that Amit used to sit next to her after returning from college and talk to her for hours. But now, all that was over. Now it was limited to greeting her when he left the house or returned home. Earlier, Amit would often ask Supriya questions and answer them himself while studying; that made Supriya feel that she was studying with him. Both of them would be jubilant if they found an answer to a difficult question. They would stay up all night before the exams.

She was very happy about Nikita and the baby to come before the marriage but soon after the marriage she had become aware of Nikita's indifference towards her.

Marriage is a bond and the happiness in a marriage depends on how well both partners understand and share the worries and joys. But Nikita chose not to acknowledge the importance of Supriya in Amit's life. Even he was too busy to give time to his sister. Amit went to the hospital, then coaching classes, then studied at home and was with Nikita all night. And so Supriya's loneliness intensified.

Whenever Nikita was getting bored or irritated, she would go to Shyam and Radhika's flat, saying that it was closer to college. Malti would bring her back each time after much cajoling. Nikita's childishness was increasing. She would fight with Malti on very small issues but would talk to her laughingly the same evening. She had no affection or sympathy for Supriya. She didn't treat her with disdain but didn't even look at her. Amit soon understood that there was a lack of empathy in Nikita.

No education is required to teach one how to give love. We always want love, but are miserly when it comes to giving it. The mathematics of love is very simple—you get as much or even more love than you give. The problem is that we fail to wait for that love. Supriya wanted to love her sister-in-law, but was confronted with her detachment. Nikita lacked the willingness to give love. Amit was worried about Supriya but never mentioned it because Nikita did not show any interest in her. Initially, he thought her silence meant an acceptance of her. But he was wrong. Nikita's behaviour had worsened after the marriage. Supriya didn't even exist for her.

It seemed that Supriya had no source of happiness, no desire to live any more. She would keep looking emptily at people all day and waiting for sleep all night. People from the neighbourhood would visit, talk to Malti, ask about Nikita's health and leave after smiling at her. She was desperate for some love from her sister-in-law. She had tried to communicate this to her through her sad face but it had no effect on Nikita. Saddened by all this, Supriya stopped eating. One night Supriya had loose motions full of blood. Malti got worried and called out to Amit. He got up immediately and gave her medicines which he always kept in the house. He, too, was worried about her and sat next to her till morning dawned. Instead of tears, there was a strange stillness in Supriya's eyes. Amit had given her attention after a very long time and she savoured it. Nikita remained lying down—it was her last month of pregnancy so they had not woken her up. Malti anyway never said anything to her but Amit was sad that she had not bothered to even ask how Supriya was.

Late in the morning when he told Nikita about Supriya, she merely commented, 'Okay, since you have given the medicines, she should be fine in some time.'

Amit was shaken; such heartlessness was difficult to understand. She enquired about her health half-heartedly, but didn't seem to hear when Amit told her Supriya's condition was serious. Supriya had high fever by the evening and her diarrhoea continued. She couldn't even drink water. Even then, Nikita had stayed in bed, staring into nothingness. When Amit saw the medicines were not working, he called an ambulance and took her to the hospital.

Glucose and steroids were administered to Supriya in the hospital but there was no improvement. It seemed that she just wanted to be freed from all ties but there was something that was holding her back. Two days passed in this way—whatever tests were conducted resulted in a blank. Even the specialists were clueless and in the end, all of them could only pray. Nikita had stayed at home but on the third day, when she missed Amit, she had come to the hospital. The moment Supriya saw Nikita, there were tears in her eyes and a smile on her face. She didn't even have the strength to move her lips. That was her last smile. Supriya had been freed of all ties, all bonds.

Malti was grief-stricken, feeling she had lost everything. Amit felt bereft, drained of all emotion. Nikita showed no reaction. Shyam and Radhika rushed to the hospital and Aditi was there too—she couldn't believe so much had happened so quickly.

There were tears in everyone's eyes except Nikita's. She was staring at everyone with stony eyes and Shyam advised Amit, 'You have lost one, don't lose the other.' Amit went to her and held her to comfort her but her eyes were vacant. Radhika took her to her own place to look after her so when the cremation took place, Amit was alone. Malti could not bear to see her beloved daughter consigned to flames so she stayed at home. Everything had changed in a day. Supriya was gone and a new member was knocking at the doors of their world.

There was silence all around when Amit reached home late at night. The bed in which Supriya was always lying was empty today. Seeing this, Amit broke down and wept uncontrollably.

34

It had been six days since Supriya passed away. Slowly, Amit and Malti were coming to terms with their loss and started looking after Nikita. Prayer services were being held at home and the seventh day, considered auspicious for the rituals, was fixed for the purpose of purifying the house.

That night Nikita's contractions began. Malti was at her side the whole night. Amit kept comforting her but Nikita continued to behave childishly, sobbing and not talking to anyone. It was around two o'clock in the night and the labour pain was increasing. The night, it seemed, would never end. Amit called up Nikita's mother who had already reached Jabalpur and they took Nikita to the hospital.

Nikita would not let Amit out of her sight even for a minute. The nurses made fun of Nikita and said, 'Madam you used to scold other patients and mothers but today you...'

'Be quiet.' Nikita scolded the nurse.

The doctor put her on a drip because of the intensifying pain. Being a student of the medical college, Nikita had been put in a special ward and was well taken care of. This was a new defining moment in the relationship Amit and Nikita shared, a new bond was about to be formed.

Then Nikita was wheeled into the delivery room. It was about an hour later when the nurse gave the happy news, 'Congratulations, Doctor! Goddess Lakshmi has arrived.'

For a second, Amit was bewildered. The moment he had eagerly waited for had finally arrived but he was clueless about what to do at that moment. When he entered the labour room, he was told that everything was fine.

Nikita looked calm. Malti told Amit, 'Congratulations! You are now a father.' Saying this, she put her hand on Amit's head.

Amit's eyes shone.

A tiny, frail, soft-as-rose-petals child was lying next to Nikita. Amit felt as if it was the rebirth of Supriya. Looking into the child's eyes, Amit's eyes were filled with tears. In a minute, motherhood had changed Nikita from a girl to a woman. Amit held her hands and felt the start of a new relationship.

Nikita could see the tears in Amit's eyes. For Amit, the old ties and relationships had gained a new meaning. This was life's new beginning.

'Hold the little one in your arms, Doctor!' said the nurse picking up the child.

When Amit looked at Nikita she signalled to him not to do so and called him near and whispered, 'Your hands are dirty, go wash them first.'

For a minute, Amit could not understand. Then he realized that the child was frail and was susceptible to infections, which is why Nikita had asked him to wash his hands. She was a doctor, after all. He smiled to himself when he thought of the love Nikita had for the child.

The circle of life is unique and nature acts in mysterious ways. One circle ends and another starts. Amit held the baby in his arms, marvelling at the tiny fingers and toes and skin as fine as dewdrops. He had been waiting for this child for so many months. He did not know whether she was Lakshmi or Saraswati; the child was his daughter.

It was the beginning of a new kind of joy. Nikita turned and kissed the baby, feeling that motherhood was an experience that was priceless, incomparable and unique.

Nikita realized that she had to protect her baby. She felt mature for the first time. She had fulfilled the role of a daughter, sister and a wife, now she was a mother. She had longed to experience this relationship for a long time. While looking at Amit, she held the child so close to her that she was barely aware that the baby had started suckling.

Amit was witnessing the entire process and was trying to understand it. He was both a part of it as well as removed from it. Nikita had given him a precious gift, which contained a part of him. The attachment was twofold—it was a mental as well as a sentimental attachment.

'Look at my stomach, he has moved from here to there.'

Amit interrupted, 'Why are you saying "he", why don't you say "she" has moved from here to there?'

The relationship between a mother and a child is the most complete relationship. It is not only emotional but related to the body and its sensations. The child remains attached to the mother as a part of her. It does not matter how the mother or the child behaves, it is but natural for a mother to understand at the touch and sound of her child what the child is feeling. But Nikita had separated herself from the role of a mother. Her mind went blank and she didn't realize when her nipple slipped out of the mouth of the baby.

Malti thought that Nikita was young and inexperienced. She asked Amit to leave the room and taught Nikita how to feed the child.

Nikita was back in the present world.

Malti came out of the room and told Amit, 'It is an auspicious occasion that a girl has been born. Today there is a prayer service for Supriya at home. We should celebrate. Faith and karma preach the same thing. Feed a Brahmin and visit Ma Durga's temple. Supriya has returned...'

There were tears of happiness in her eyes.

35

AMIT was extremely happy. The sorrow of losing Supriya was displaced by the arrival of the child. She was named Akanksha. The house was filled with happiness. Amit was preparing for his MD exams and had to sit up all night studying. Nikita would remain sleeping. Whenever Akanksha cried at night, Amit and Ma would take turns to pacify the child. Nikita would never get up. Amit noticed that sometimes Akanksha would be lying next to Nikita crying and Nikita would be staring into space. Sometimes she would be silent and at times would be found playing with Akanksha. If she were laughing, she would laugh the whole day and if she went silent, silence would prevail. Sometimes Nikita would talk to Malti the whole day and at times, she wouldn't talk to her at all.

Amit noticed not only a change in Nikita's attitude but also her quirky behaviour. Before going off to sleep, Nikita would ask Amit to wash his hands. Even when Amit washed his hands, Nikita would not believe him until he washed his hands again.

Nikita would often lose her temper. One day, Malti had only talked to her about Supriya and the birth of Akanksha, whom she saw as a reincarnation of Supriya. Nikita suddenly got very angry. She yelled, cried and cursed Malti.

'You want my daughter to be crippled like yours?' she screamed.

Malti started crying and Amit was shocked.

The moment Amit rebuked her, Nikita snubbed him by saying, 'Go to your mother, don't come near me...'

Nikita went out of control and the women in the neighbourhood witnessed the entire incident. Everyone tried to reason with her but to no avail. She kept on screaming. Her irrational behaviour became a topic of discussion in the neighbourhood.

Amit had spent his life peacefully and with respect even when faced with poverty. He had earned a life of dignity through his hard work. But that day he felt he and Nikita had fallen into an abyss. Amit couldn't sleep the whole night, but Nikita was in a deep slumber. When Akanksha started crying, Amit picked her up and gave her to Malti, who soothed the baby. She had not slept either; the insult had hurt her badly. She could not see where she had gone wrong.

Nikita got up late. She talked to Malti as if nothing had happened the previous night. Amit left for the hospital, determined to forgive Nikita. Perhaps it was the love for her daughter that made Nikita react to Malti's words. Slowly, time erased this memory and the days went by slowly.

However, that incident made Amit and Malti, in days to come, approach Nikita with caution.

A television had entered their home. Slowly other things that were required by Nikita were bought. But Nikita wasn't satisfied staying at home. She hadn't tried her hand at cooking. The whole day she would either watch television or keep lying around. The internship at the college was progressing slowly and Nikita sometimes used to go to college. Amit had told her to start practising in the hospital, to follow her profession. Nikita wasn't interested. To help her talk to her parents in Delhi, a telephone had been installed at home. She used to talk at least twice a week but after the telephonic conversation, her behaviour became distant. She wouldn't compromise even on small things. Peculiar ideas used to clog her mind. Amit tried to talk her out of them but she would still think in a strange way, making her distant from others.

Amit, after consulting Shyam and Rajesh, had bought a scooter on instalments. He thought it would be convenient while going out with Nikita, but she did not want to stir, refusing to go out. Several thoughts surrounded Amit. Nikita used to go out frequently before they got married, then why not now?...Was he at fault?... These thoughts lead him to feeling inferior. That Nikita was suffering from a mental disease was difficult for him to accept. He could never think on those lines. Once or twice Amit noticed that while in the market, Nikita would lose her temper. Be it in the market or on the scooter, she would continue to rave and rant. Sometimes Amit would interrupt and that would escalate the situation. People gathered to stare, a curious audience at times. Amit felt scared talking to her. The expenses were increasing and Amit was working hard to keep up with them. Akanksha was growing older but Amit could not be a part of her childhood as he should have been.

Once Malti came back from school and said to Amit and Nikita, 'The principal of my school, Guruji and his wife are coming over... especially to meet Nikita and Akanksha...' Her tone was that of a request. 'They have been of great help in times of need.'

Malti wanted to tell her more about Guruji but Nikita was not interested.

Amit also tried to talk about Guruji but Nikita snapped and said, 'Why are mother and son being so obsequious...!'

The sharp and distant tone made Amit angry. Didn't he have the right to speak in the house?

Nikita started again, 'Have my people ever been invited?'

Amit could not understand how the matter had gained a new meaning. He thought about it, thinking that even if he's never invited them, they never visited either. Even during the wedding, they were not happy. He felt that her parents did not like him. Nikita had never mentioned this earlier otherwise he would have happily invited them over. It was no use arguing and Amit tried to calm her by saying, 'We will invite them for sure.'

'No, you won't. You have never invited them. You are always concerned about your family. Your sister, your mother, her school... all shoddy people.' After saying all this, she started crying.

Amit could not understand why she had reacted so violently and became worried.

Malti said simply, 'Nikita is right. We have never invited her people over nor has she visited them. You should take her to meet them.'

'But Ma, we never got the opportunity to visit them. We gave them the news regarding Supriya and Akanksha but…' Amit went silent.

Nikita answered back, 'They lead very busy lives. What will you know about Delhi life! Do you think they will come running for small matters? How many times do you go to see them?'

Amit's anger was increasing. Death is a small matter for them, Akanksha's birth is a small matter for them, then what is important? Moreover, they have also never invited us. But, he remained silent. Guruji was coming over and the matter could worsen. Amit could not understand how such a small thing had gained in proportion like this.

Malti was taken aback. She had started feeling guilty. It would have been better if they had not asked to visit them. Now that she had said yes, she could not cancel the plan. Moreover, she had praised Nikita a lot in front of him and it was not like they had visitors every day. Kamla would come sometimes but Gita and Usha hardly paid a visit. And she used to be preoccupied with Akansksha, school and home.

Nikita rested the whole day. Malti never let her live in discomfort. Even today, Malti patiently asked Nikita to calm down and finally, Nikita relaxed.

Guruji arrived with his wife in the evening. He was retired now. His wife was quite a chatterbox. Amit touched both Guruji and his wife's feet. Guruji's wife kept talking to Malti and playing with Akanksha, saying, 'Such a pretty child.' Malti was relieved. The wife hadn't seen Supriya so did not take her name but Amit and Supriya resembled each other. The wife after closely looking at the child said, 'She has gone on her father, she is lucky!'

Nikita's expression had changed. Malti tried to save the situation by saying, 'The face of a child keeps changing—she will be as beautiful as her mother. I am lucky to have her as my daughter-in-law.'

Nikita did not say a word. She did not smile or say anything. In the end when the guests left Amit heaved a sigh of relief.

36

NIKITA'S undefined, uncontrolled and abrupt behaviour became worse. Till now Amit was not thinking of it as a disease but as a part of her behaviour. He was saddened by this and Malti was afraid of it.

One day, she went to the market to shop. Amit was returning from the hospital. On seeing Nikita in the shop, he stopped. Thinking that both of them would go back home on the scooter, he went into the shop to buy things for himself. He asked Nikita, 'Is there anything else you want to buy?'

Nikita, without looking at Amit, asked the shopkeeper, 'How much do I have to pay?'

'Should I give you the total of both your purchases?'

'Why is that? I need to know the amount for what I have bought,' said Nikita in a sharp tone.

The shopkeeper smiled at Nikita, charged her the required amount and said to Amit, 'It seems she is angry.'

Nikita went back home without even looking at Amit.

Amit was shocked. He had never felt so humiliated as today by the shopkeeper's remark and smile.

Nikita's strange behaviour continued. It became a common recurrence in the neighbourhood. Amit was under stress. He could not understand what was happening. What mistake had he made? He had sleepless nights. Sometimes he had to feed Akanksha because Nikita wouldn't—she was not even a year old. Thinking that Nikita was stubborn by nature was all he could conclude.

Nikita would do what she felt like. She would not miss even one opportunity to show disrespect. Whatever Amit and Malti used to say, she would do just the opposite. But why? Amit didn't have any answers.

Nikita would start fighting even without a reason. Amit would get irritated but would gently try to make her understand. Sometimes without being at fault, he would apologize simply to calm her down.

But that did not affect Nikita, her anger could be triggered off by the slightest thing. Her behaviour had an uneven pattern.

With time, Amit noticed that Nikita would be lost in her own thoughts. Sometimes she was unhappy, at other times extremely cheerful. When she was normal, she would talk to Akanksha and love her but at other times, would not pay her any attention. Sometimes she would beat her up and scream at her.

Whenever Malti tried to take Akanksha away from this, she would be subjected to angry words as well.

Whenever Nikita wanted love from Amit, she would force herself on him. Although Amit was still in love with her and physically attracted to her, the mental instability had started affecting him. In times of intimacy, he could not enjoy their physical contact nor did he feel connected.

An incident on one particular night left him speechless. Nikita had put Akanksha next to Malti and had made Amit wash his hands several times saying, 'Your hands are dirty, you should come near me only when your hands are clean.'

Every day Amit used to wash his hands but this night he was confused.

Later, Nikita said, 'I want a child.' Amit said, 'Is Akanksha not your child?'

'She is your child, I want a child who resembles me.'

Amit felt angry after hearing this but Nikita tried to get him to make love to her. Nikita started screaming when he didn't respond. Amit got scared and tried to make her understand, 'Speak softly, everyone can hear you. Ma and the neighbours can hear you.'

But she kept screaming, 'You people don't know how to love. I am so unlucky. All of you want to kill me...'

Amit put his hand on her mouth so that the noise would not

reach outside but she kept screaming, 'Now you want to throttle me?'

Suddenly, Amit heard someone whispering through the door, 'Is everything all right? Is she okay?'

'Nothing Ma, everything is fine.'

Amit held her in her arms so that she would not make a noise but Nikita started kissing his bare arms.

Every day Nikita would try to get him to bed, saying she wanted a baby. When Nikita became pregnant again, Amit could not even react properly to the news. Still, he tried to search for happiness in Nikita's happiness.

There would be times when he needed his wife to listen to him, to talk about his problems, but he was afraid of talking to Nikita. Nothing he did was right—even gifts he got for her were rejected.

Nikita found faults with everything. Nature's beauty and picnic spots held no fascination for her. Movies, shopping, interacting with people held no interest for her. She used to be lost in her own world.

The neighbourhood women stayed away from her and now Amit dreaded coming back home. But where was Malti to go?

37

THE saying that when pain exceeds its limit, it acts as a medicine, does not always hold true. However, it does find a way out. Malti was a very simple-minded person and didn't talk much. If God had given her pain, he had bestowed her with as much resilience. Earlier, she was spared from the gossip of the neighbourhood because of her work in the school and now her life revolved around Akanksha. Supriya had come back to her life in a new form.

Life goes on. Akanksha's existence brought a new energy to Malti. She found Supriya in her and found happiness in this.

Amit, too, was an optimist and was used to struggle and hard work to achieve his goals. He had his whole life in front of him. He was under a lot of stress but that had not broken him yet. A sensitive and a sentimental person values his respect in society a lot. Gossip about Nikita and him in the neighbourhood used to hurt him. He never discussed his problems with his friends as he felt that this was his family issue and didn't want people to know. Maybe there was a problem with him, and if that was the case, that too needed to be resolved. After giving it a lot of thought, he went to a psychiatrist, Dr Chaudhary, one day.

Looking into his eyes, the doctor said, 'Yes, tell me what your problem is.' He did not know where to start—how much to tell, how much to hide. All he could say was, 'There is no happiness left in my marriage. I want to know the reason. My wife's behaviour is not the same. She is well educated, a doctor, but nothing is right.'

'Where is your wife? Maybe she, too, has complaints about you. Until I hear both sides, I cannot help you. Bring her along. And as you have already told me, she is a doctor, so that should not be a problem.'

At night, Amit lovingly took Nikita in his arms and said, 'Nikita, I haven't given you any happiness. It might be that something is wrong with me. You haven't said anything but you are not happy. Do you know, I had a talk with a doctor and he said that after understanding the situation he will try to do something about it. You have to come along with me, please.'

'Do you think I am crazy?'

'No, no. I meant about myself. If you won't tell me what it is about me that you can't tolerate, how will I know?'

'Then the mother and the son should go and take the daughter along,' said Nikita in a sharp tone and went off to sleep. Amit was shocked, but he did not lose hope. He again went to the doctor and asked for advice.

Instead of giving advice, the doctor gave him a long lecture, 'These days most marriages are unsuccessful. There are many reasons for it. For ages, men and their families have exploited women and it continues till date. In the present scenario, women have become alert. Knowingly or unknowingly, the girl's family gives advice to the girl and since the girl is educated, independent and self-sufficent, they do not compromise. Before she is old enough, she is independent and the husband's name hardly features on her priority list. Matters related to sex are another problem. It is a necessary and an important relationship between a husband and a wife. Due to various reasons if one of them is not happy, there is a problem. Mental stress can cause a loss of interest in sex for men. On the other hand, women now know more about their bodies and their needs...' The doctor took a deep breath and continued, 'There are many reasons for a disturbed marriage and you are not alone. Now what is your reason and what can you do in such a situation is for you to see and find out. A family is based on relations and relations are based on ties. Ties in which there are no feelings, make love and trust casualties. For feelings, love and trust, the heart must triumph over the mind.'

After hearing this Amit thought the doctor was right. 'You are absolutely right! Can you help me? If you have belief in me, I will tell you everything correctly. There is no room for lies.' Amit told the doctor about Nikita's behaviour. The doctor heard everything carefully and then said, 'If you are telling me everything truthfully then there is something wrong. It can be a mental disorder, but without meeting the patient I cannot say anything.'

Amit suddenly said, 'No, No ! That's impossible!'

The doctor was moved and said, 'It seems you love your wife a lot. What do you want? Maybe I can help.'

'I want her to be happy but she is not happy.'

'Have you visited her parents?'

'No, I have never been invited to visit them. Their behaviour towards me is cold. Maybe I am not worth it.'

'You should visit them. You should do what your wife likes.'

'But she doesn't like anything.'

'That is not possible. Search. Try giving her a conducive environment. Perhaps a change of scene will work, away from the present environment. Take a house in another place. If possible, go on a vacation.'

'And her behaviour towards Akanksha?' asked Amit.

'It is possible that you may have hurt her. That is why she considers everything connected to you a reason for her unhappiness. However this should not happen. Make her understand in a loving manner. Maybe she will understand after her second child. It is possible that there might have been a shock before marriage, although science does not prove shock as a reason for mental disorder. It can be depression. Still I can't say anything till I see her. Only she will know the reason. Do what I have told you to. If possible, I would like to see her. She seems to be suffering from depression. But the reason needs to be found.'

What could he do now? Nikita was pregnant again, she had to be looked after. He would talk to Ma about the new house. Commuting from college was difficult and why was it necessary for Ma to work in school? If it was about money, then he would work in the evenings at the hospital.

Soon Amit got a two-room house in Shastri Nagar. Shyam and Radhika were very happy because their house was nearby. Amit got to know that Radhika was the daughter of an influential businessman, a fact Radhika had never mentioned nor made apparent. Radhika's family had gifted her a luxury car as a wedding present. Shyam's parents were influential landlords in a village and her parents were a highly respectable family of Delhi. The two families met often in Jabalpur and had an excellent rapport.

One day Radhika and Shyam came over and Nikita was happy to see them. Looking at the car, Nikita asked, 'When did you buy this?'

Radhika said, 'Papa gifted it.'

Shyam added jokingly, 'Came as dowry.'

Nikita asked, 'Your parents visit you?'

Radhika answered, 'Yes, they come often.'

'You must be inviting them?' Nikita was in a mood to talk.

'No, no, what invitation? They come themselves. I am their daughter, but yes I do invite my in-laws and they visit themselves as well. What about your parents?'

'They are busy.' said Nikita in a sad tone.

'Okay this time all of us must visit Shyam's village in the car,' said Radhika in an excited tone. She enjoyed the company of friends.

'Ask Nikita,' said Amit, looking at her nervously.

'Let's go. It will be fun,' said Radhika, holding Nikita's hand.

'Okay we will go,' said Nikita slowly, nodding her head.

38

NEXT Sunday, everyone, including Akanksha, went to Narsinghpur. They insisted that Malti also come along with them but she refused and said, 'No, you young ones should go. I will come along another time.' Nikita did not ask her even once. Radhika kept on saying, 'You will enjoy yourself with everyone around.' But Malti did not agree.

Nikita did not care about Akanksha throughout the journey. Amit kept holding her all the time while Nikita looked out of the window. If Akanksha cried, Amit would quieten her. Radhika couldn't resist asking, 'What is wrong? You two are not talking? Why so silent?' The conversation had just started when Akanksha started crying and Amit tried to calm her. In the end he gave up.

Nikita grabbed Akanksha and shook her till she stopped crying. There was fear in her innocent eyes. Amit was filled with love for the child and took her in his lap. The moment Akanksha was on his lap, she started crying again. In between she would look at Nikita with fear. How could a one-year-old child understand her mother's behaviour? After some time she went off to sleep on her father's lap. Radhika and Shyam found this strange. On reaching home, Radhika got busy talking to her in-laws. Nikita was feeling restless. Shyam's family took good care of Akanksha and Nikita. They wouldn't leave Akanksha even for a minute but Nikita did not speak at all. Even at dinner, she was silent. After dinner when everyone was sitting in the garden, Nikita started insisting on going back home. Shyam was surprised and said, 'We have just arrived. Stay for a day at least.'

'No, you people stay, we will leave...Amit, I want to go home in the morning.'

Shyam tried to convince her to stay but Nikita did not listen. In the end, Amit brought Nikita back home by train. Once they were home, he gave a deep sigh. There were several questions related to last night that were rising in his mind but keeping them suppressed, he only said, 'If you did not feel like going, then we shouldn't have ventured out at all.'

'Why? If you were enjoying yourself then you should have stayed there. Friends matter to you, not us.' Nikita started screaming. She picked up her slippers and threw them on the floor. Malti got scared. What had happened? She was fine when she had left. Afraid that she would harm herself in her state of pregnancy, Amit caught hold of Nikita but Nikita hit her head against the wall and yelled, 'You want to kill me?'

Nikita's head was bleeding. Amit quickly got band-aid and Dettol. He would have bandaged her wound but Nikita kept screaming. Akanksha stared at her, terrified, and then shut her eyes as if to block her out. Malti requested her with folded hands, 'Please forgive Amit if he has done anything wrong...you should be careful in this condition.'

'You want my child dead! Your daughter came back to kill me!'

'Are you crazy?' yelled Amit. He felt awful seeing his mother with folded hands for no fault of hers. Then words about Supriya enraged him. He raised his hand and slapped Nikita hard. For a minute there was silence, but Nikita went crazy. She attacked Amit, slapping him back, pushing him to the door. 'Get out! You hit me? You bastards don't know how to talk to a girl...you will hit me? Yes...hit me!' And pushing him out, she locked the door. Malti was still inside and Akanksha could be heard crying loudly. Nikita's foul words were spilling out on the streets, hurting Amit like shards of glass. He tried to avoid the stares of the people on the road.. Crossing the road, he reached a paan shop and asked for a cigarette, feeling he needed to calm his jangled nerves. 'I live nearby, I have forgotten to get the money. I will pay you.' The shopkeeper looked at him closely and gave him the cigarette. When the guilt overcame anger, introspection started—Amit felt he should not have hit her at any cost, but then he thought, 'How could Nikita talk in that insane way?' But he realized he did not have the right to hit her. In the end he made up his mind to apologize to Nikita. On his way back he kept thinking about his mother who had never seen happiness. Reaching home, he found the door open. Nikita had locked herself inside her room, Akanksha was lying on her bed and Malti was in the kitchen. They did not look at each other. When Amit embraced his daughter, she tried to hide her face. When at last Nikita opened her door, Amit apologized profusely, and Nikita was quiet.

Amit took Nikita to Delhi, hoping it would make her feel better. Everyone was at home—her brother and his wife, his sister and her parents. This time they treated Amit well. One day on seeing sleeping pills and anti-depressant medicines, Amit asked Pranita, Nikita's sister, 'Who takes these tablets?'

'Papa, when he is unable to sleep,' she said.

One evening when Amit had been given his tea, Nikita's mother asked, 'How has Nikita been?'

'She is like a stubborn child,' said Amit in a playful manner. Nikita frowned at him. Suddenly she started yelling, 'I have ruined my life by marrying into this family. He and his mother pretend to be innocent. But all the time his mother keeps inciting him against me. Both mother and son trouble me the whole day. What else to expect from small people from small towns. Even their thinking is narrow. They don't know how to behave with their daughter-in-law.' Nikita's words were like arrows which wounded him. He felt like running away but Akanksha was there and she was crying. Nikita's mother said in a normal tone, 'We have people living nearby. Nikita, speak softly. What will people think? Go to your own home and then fight. You have made your own choices.'

'That is why I am saying my life is ruined! They want to kill me,' saying this she started crying. Her mother and sister tried to calm her down. No one bothered about Amit. He was taken aback—what had happened in just a minute? Today he was not angry but felt defeated. He was on the verge of a breakdown. He had no energy to think or act. At one's in-laws' one got respect and love but here he faced insults beyond comprehension. But why? What was his fault? Why did his mother-in-law let him get insulted? Normally Amit was a calm person but being insulted in front of everyone, he felt broken. He could never forget this incident his whole life. He could never understand why he was insulted. He had witnessed Nikita's behaviour before. But the audience to this insult could have stopped her, at least scolded her. She was their daughter, it would have its effect. Didn't he have an identity? No respect? Was he not worth Nikita or her family? Despite being educated, a doctor, was he of no use? He wanted to tell her family that he did not trap her, but then he remained silent.

Nikita suddenly began behaving as if nothing had happened. When they left, the mother-in-law gifted Amit a shirt and a sari for his mother. He quietly took them and bid them goodbye. On the way back, Nikita kept praising her family but Amit kept quiet. As a compensation for the insult he had been given a shirt and a sari! For once he laughed to himself and resolved never to go to Delhi. Why go to a place where there was no love and only disrespect.

39

He had very little recollection of when Aniruddh was born. He did not even register when Akanksha grew up. The childhood of his children, the pleasures of marriage, love from in-laws, life's happiness—none of these seemed to exist for him. Remembering his own childhood, he did not recollect great unhappiness nor happiness, but there was a burning desire to live, to be alive. He never ran away from problems and tried to solve them. But he could not tolerate his mother's suffering.

Nikita never felt she was doing anything wrong so she would never apologize for her behaviour. Malti would listen silently to her ranting and raving, trying to hide her emotions. She could not see her son suffer. She looked after the house, cooked and looked after the children—she had brought up Akanksha. She talked to her granddaughter but never mentioned Supriya, scared that it would provoke Nikita. At the same time, she would keep telling Amit, 'Take care of the children, they are growing up. They need you.'

Nikita somehow finished her MBBS and Amit, his MD. He did not want to study further. He enjoyed working at the hospital, enjoyed talking to patients, listening to their problems and trying to give advice. He was a favourite. All his friends had left Jabalpur. Aditi had finished her Master's and gone abroad. Shyam and Radhika had finished their postgraduate studies and had gone to Delhi to practise. Because of Nikita's behaviour, they had avoided visiting Amit when they were in Jabalpur. They met Amit at college instead and did not even mention her name to spare him the torture. But they understood his troubles. Other friends were unable to finish their postgraduation in the first attempt, so some went to other colleges while others started their private practice. The parents of some fortunate ones opened a clinic for them while others were gaining experience by practising in other clinics. Wrapped up in his own world, Vikram had finished his MBBS and gone away, no one knew where.

Amit sat for the UPSC railways exam and cleared it. His first posting was in Bhusawal (in Maharashtra). Malti refused to go along. She explained to him. 'It's a new life. Go alone. Enjoy yourself, may be that is what Nikita wants and would like. You are tied down because of me. I will keep visiting and if you are happy then I'm happy too.' He had cleared the all-India class I exam and had become a doctor but there were no celebrations at home, nor were any sweet dishes made. Malti was afraid of doing anything in the new house. She could not move out of the house because she hadn't even seen her neighbourhood. Diwali and Holi passed. Malti moved back to Darjani mohalla. She did not need money and she had no desires. The neighbourhood was happy to have Malti back. Many advised Amit to stay and work at the Jabalpur railway hospital but he wanted to practise elsewhere.

Amit reached Bhusawal along with his wife and kids. It is a small city on the banks of the Tapti river. For the Indian Railways, it was a very important station, with Mumbai on one side, Delhi on another and Nagpur on the third side. It was the main office of the independent central division of the railways and the divisional railway manager's office and the centre were established here. The Jabalpur division was also established here. Amit got a huge bungalow near the Tapti.

In the beginning, Nikita seemed happy. There were servants living in the servant's quarters. Slowly Amit's hard work brought him fame and on Amit's advice, Nikita had started practising at a private clinic. Nikita did not like visitors nor was she friendly with anyone, finding fault with everyone. And her insistence on making Amit wash his hands frequently persisted. Amit sometimes got fed up. She loved Aniruddh but then she would often go blank, sitting for hours doing nothing. Another oddity was that she would take things only from the left hand—if anyone gave her something from the right hand, she would start fighting.

Nikita was not inclined to cook and hardly went to the kitchen. She did not like going to the private clinic and Amit never forced her. She preferred to be in her bedroom the whole day, spending very little time in their beautiful garden. In thc evening, people would go on a stroll near the Tapti but Nikita would stay at home, while Amit was at the hospital. The Maharashtrian maid who lived in the servant quarters used to cook their food, but Nikita would not allow her inside the house sometimes when she was in a strange mood and no food was cooked for days. Amit would go to the hospital hungry and the children would suffer. Amit would secretly give them milk and biscuits and he started keeping dry food at home. He was now looking after the house and bought the groceries as well. Raising Akanksha was now his responsibility. Due to the absence of Malti, the condition of the children was deteriorating.

Once she told Amit, 'Akanksha is grown up. It is difficult to make love with her around. She should sleep in another room.'

Amit said, 'She is only five years old and children have a deep sleep. Besides we hardly make love.'

But negative thoughts started dominating her mind. One night she started screaming, 'Make her sleep in another room. She will kill me!' In the end Amit gave in and a bed was placed in another room.

Akanksha was very young and got frightened. How could she sleep alone in the huge rooms of these houses built in the British era? She was awfully scared. On seeing her father leave, she screamed. Amit rushed back into the room and hugged her. Akanksha was scared and looked at her father with innocent eyes. Amit felt that she was trying to understand his helplessness. Ridden by emotions, he decided to sleep in that room.

But the second night, Nikita created a scene. 'You only love your daughter. If I die, you wouldn't care.' And then she slapped Akanksha.

The very next day, Amit requested Malti to come and live with them. At least Akanksha would be taken care of and the children would be fed. It was a relief when she arrived. But Nikita's condition worsened. Tormented, Amit consulted a psychiatrist at the hospital.

Dr Anand was a kind man. After listening to Amit he decided to pay a visit to their home. Nikita was made to sit with him for tea and Amit quietly left the room. The doctor talked to her and then made three more visits. Then he called Amit and said, 'She is schizophrenic. It will be a long treatment.' He prescribed sedatives and advised Amit to handle her with a lot of love and to ensure a stress-free atmosphere at home. While talking to Dr Anand, Amit told him about Nikita's father taking anti-depressants, knowing that family hisory was important in a case like Nikita's.

Amit was worried after hearing of Nikita's ailment...how would he manage? He had to do it alone. Akanksha and Amit were growing up and he had to take care of them. Nikita's heavy medication made her even more sleepy so she could not take care of the children. He had no expectations from his in-laws, who seemed to instigate her to fight with him when they called her. He wondered what they talked about! Malti was unhappy and went back to Jabalpur frequently. After a lot of thinking, Amit got himself transferred to the Jabalpur railway hospital. His city. People knew him and his mother would stay with him. Whenever she missed her home, she could visit the neighbourhood. The children would be taken care of and at the medical college, the treatment would be good. A positive development was that Amit was promoted to the post of divisional medical officer.

That is how Amit came back to Jabalpur. And today, at that same hospital, he had been admitted as a patient. Amit opened his eyes to see Aditi talking to Akanksha and Aniruddh. It was dark outside. On hearing him move, the three looked at him and came up to his bed. He called Akanksha and Aniruddh to him and asked yet again, 'How is your mother?'

'She is fine,' said Aniruddh, lowering his eyes.

'You are grown up. Take care of yourselves.'

'Yes.'

'Now you two go home, it is getting late. You need to study. If you want you can come here after school.' He gazed at them with love in his eyes.

Amit sent them home. Aditi was happy to see their relationship. 'You love them a lot, don't you?' she asked, smiling.

'Hmmm'

'How are you?'

'I am fine.'

'Ma was worried. She was remembering Malti Aunty. Don't worry. Your children are strong and can look after themselves. You'll get well too.'

Aditi stroked Amit's head. Amit couldn't understand if this was a doctor's concern or a friend's, but the touch felt good.

'Don't think too much. Last night you must have been worried.'

Aditi continued, 'Look at me—lonely, living with a widowed mother. Facing so many troubles yet not giving up. What do I have? Nothing for the future. But I am not worried...I am not fighting but living.'

He could relate to Aditi emotionally. Suddenly, she changed the topic and said, 'Your children are your future. They are lovely. They were close to their grandmother and loved her a lot. They were missing her. Malti Aunty was very calm, loving and full of motherly affection. You never told me about her—you should have informed me.'

While talking, Aditi noticed that the drip had finished. She removed it and told the nurse to take care of him. While going out of the room, she said, 'I will come in the morning with tea. You must rest now and don't worry at all.'

40

AMIT kept thinking the whole night. He felt that he had been wrong about Aditi. She had retained the childhood tie they shared without any strings attached. She remembered Ma as well. She was right in saying that the children were close to their grandmother and why not, she had brought them up. She was a caring grandmother and her entire old age had been dedicated to his children. Today he felt the absence of Ma. If she was there, she would have been with him in the hospital. Memories enveloped him. Remembering Ma increased the pain. What did she get in reward for her goodness? All her life she had suffered. When he was in Bhusawal, away from Jabalpur, she was here alone. Alone in her old age. No work to do, no aims, no desires. He used to send her money every month, hiding it from Nikita, afraid of her sharp tongue. Whatever she said acted like arrows wounding him. Then he would tell himself not to get affected by it, reminding himself that she was ill.

Returning to Jabalpur was the right step. At least his mother was with him and the kids were being taken care of. He was less worried about them. Now only Nikita's mood swings were a source of worry, following a cycle of ups and downs. Nikita would abuse the children, making Malti cry internally and Akanksha would cry looking at her grandmother's condition. Malti would hide a lot of Nikita's behaviour from Amit but fear had set in Akanksha's mind. Even as a child, she got scared and quickly agreed with whatever her mother said. The moment her mother would leave, she would cling to her grandmother and cry. She would sleep next to her grandmother and when she could not handle her mother's temper, she would hide behind her. This had turned Akanksha's into a quiet and introverted girl.

At times she missed school because she had to look after the house as well. On her grandmother's instructions, she took care of Amit. His morning tea and his clothes were laid out by her. She served him food as well. She was a backbencher at school and be it studies or sports, she did not participate in any school events. She loved and was attached to her younger brother, Aniruddh, who spent most of his time with his grandmother. He did not like hearing Nikita curse his sister and his grandmother and often got angry with his mother—he was the only one she could not bear hurting. When she would make Akanksha wash her hands several times, Aniruddh would snap at her and Nikita wouldn't say a word to him. Aniruddh was good at studies but was worried because of the circumstances at home. He became stubborn and irritable. He loved his father but didn't like the way he let Nikita say cruel things to his sister and grandmother. He could not understand his father's lack of reaction. Nikita remained under the influence of medicines for many years. After coming back from Bhusawal, the treatment was going on fine. She would be in her own world, would scream less and was less angry. She hardly came out of her room and did not like outsiders. If she ever went out, she would return early. When she was fine, she would talk to Malti and to the children and even go to the market but the unpredictable mood swings would set in suddenly, making her a different person. The children kept their distance from her and at night would sleep next to their grandmother.

One day Malti told Amit, 'Take care, Akanksha is growing up.'

He did not understand. She hesistantly told him, 'She is growing up...her periods have started.' He looked at Akanksha, thinking how this fragile girl had grown up without him noticing. Akanksha loved her father but whenever she would talk to him, there was fear and hesitation and perhaps that was the reason why they didn't know each other well.

'Amit, please ask someone to explain the process to her and what she should do...in the modern way.'

He felt guilty that his mother had to talk to him about such things. Late at night, he went to his daughter and stroked her head. Akanksha was awake. Fear and shame were evident on her face. She could not meet her father's eyes. She felt like sitting with him for a long time, listening to him and she felt protected. She held on to her feelings in her clenched fists.

She heard footsteps, on slowly opening her eyes she found her father leaving the room. The moment he left, her feelings came out in the form of tears.

Amit used to get sanitary napkins for Nikita but now he had to secretly get them for his daughter and he felt ashamed. He did not know how Nikita would react and so out of fear he did not tell her about it. He felt strange doing this. Quietly, he got the napkins and gave them to his mother. Akanksha turned more quiet, her personality becoming subdued. She did not feel like coming out of the kitchen. The only person she could act stubbornly with was her grandmother, whom she sometimes quarrelled with.

41

AKANKSHA and Aniruddh were emotionally attached to their grandmother but till the end they could not understand what connected them to her. Aniruddh would fight with her, be angry, say something but their grandmother saw love even in that. Akanksha was once participating in a cultural programme at her convent school. She wanted the entire family to come and see her, especially her grandmother. She was just a child and insisted on this. 'Why will Dadi not come along? She has to see me on stage.'

'How can Dadi come? She is not well.'

'She is all right,' and she looked at her smiling grandmother expectantly.

At that time, Nikita was well due to medicines.

In the room, her grandmother had tried to make her understand that she did not understand English and her friends would look down on her but Akanksha would not listen.

'Why don't you make her understand? What will Ma do there? Is it necessary for everyone to go?' Nikita's tone was changing. Her beautiful eyes had changed expression. Amit realized that if her condition worsened, it would be difficult to handle the situation. At least Nikita was coming to school. On Nikita's insistence, he scolded Akanksha and even slapped her. Akanksha got scared and did not know what she had done to make her father angry. Thus, in the end, Malti did not go, but Aniruddh went with them. While leaving, she looked at grandmother with a scared look in her eyes. It was her first and last programme in school. She forgot everything on the stage and people laughed at her. The programme was ruined. Instead of sympathizing, Nikita started scolding her, 'I have always told your father that such a useless girl could not be my child.'

Amit felt sorry for his daughter and he could not forgive himself for slapping her.

Most of the time, Malti would solve her grandchildren's problems but this time she could not read their faces. The moment she saw Akanksha, she took her in her arms and said, 'Today you must have been really good. Everyone must have been calling out your name…' Taking the conversation further, she asked, 'Who was the hero?' She tried to tease her and could not understand why Akanksha was quiet and sad. She kept saying, 'Oh, tell me, what did you do on stage?'

After listening to this for some time, Nikita yelled from her room, 'This is all you teach kids. Slowly everyone will become my enemy. Although she is not my daughter, I was humiliated. A woman from the neighbourhood smiled at me—you people must have told her to do it. The guard was glaring at me. You people must have told him about me.'

Saying this, she flew at Akanksha and began slapping her. Malti was shocked. Akanksha was about to faint. Amit saved her by snatching her from Nikita's clutches and took her away. Akanksha couldn't go to school for a few days and couldn't sleep at night. It broke her grandmother's heart to see her sadness and shame.

After a few months, it was Aniruddh's sports day and he was participating. On sports day, forgetting his sister's experience, Aniruddh started insisting, 'Dadi, you have to come. You don't need to understand a language to follow sports. I am participating in the races.'

'I don't know how to run,' she tried to dissuade him.

'You can watch me run,' said Aniruddh.

'No, beta, I am not feeling well.' Malti hadn't forgotten the last incident. She hadn't come out of the shock of that day and really wasn't well. Nikita knew that she couldn't scold Aniruddh. She said, 'You are not happy when the children are happy. If he is asking you then why don't you come along?'

Malti did not know what to do. Everything was topsy turvy.

She did not know what was going on in Nikita's mind. She went to the school but did not say a word, fearful of how it would affect Nikita. On their way back, Aniruddh sat with Akanksha and his grandmother, happily holding on to his participation certificate. The family was together, but Nikita was mumbling, 'No one knows how to be happy when the children are happy.' Malti remained silent.

42

'I wonder when I'll ever get freedom,' the thought kept crossing Amit's mind. Honesty may be laudable but some things have to remain concealed.

The ties that bind are those of love. The ties that are forced are painful. There is no difference between such ties and a prison. The definitions of ties and those that bind us keep changing.

Amit accepted Nikita's state and all the sorrow she caused, but there was a limit to it. Amit and Malti were very tolerant of people. But such a quality depends on the situation, time and place for it can become a fault. Nikita's illness was a truth but was it acceptable at the cost of the loss of other people's identities? As the days went by she treated Malti with contempt, not even bothering to talk to her. In fact, she seemed to look at her as an enemy.

Malti's health was deteriorating—she had intense diarrhoea and was incontinent. To call Lakshmi in the middle of the night was not feasible, so Amit and Akanksha cleaned her up. Nikita was unable to sleep and began grumbling. He knew it was no use telling her that Malti was in a bad state. He knew it would spell trouble. Looking at Nikita's mental condition, he did not know whether anything could be said to her. Also, if the person did not listen to what you had to say, there was no question of a conversation. There are several ways to understand relationships. Love for parents, for someone close and even childhood connections create bonds which cannot be explained. There is another kind of a bond, which is accepted without thinking or feeling. A tie where a person feels like a prisoner and wants to get out of it but can't. Such ties hold people back. But he felt there were no ties binding Nikita.

Malti's body had given up and she became bedridden. Her

appetite vanished and her will to live diminished progressively. The medicines stopped having any effect. Lakshmi used to clean up at times but it was Akanksha who cleaned up her grandmother every day. Nikita merely muttered, 'It would be better if she passes away.'

Amit was unhappy to see his mother suffer. As a child, when he was ill, she would be up all night to take care of him.

Since Aniruddh had been brought up by his grandmother, he wanted to be with her but Nikita kept him away. Still, he would go to his grandmother whenever he could. Akanksha took care of her in a reversal of roles, paying her grandmother for the way she had looked after her as a child. When Malti would see her clean up, she would bless her from her heart. However, until Akanksha came back from school, she would be lying in her soiled bed. Amit told Nikita time and again, 'We should keep a ward boy to take care of her.' But Nikita refused to listen and kept deferring it. Nikita could never see herself in such a situation and Amit was sad that his mother had to face this suffering. What she had done for them was beyond the ties that bound them, going beyond the call of duty to look after her grandchildren. He could understand how much his mother wanted to be released from suffering. She wanted release from the ties with a son, daughter-in-law and grandchildren and her wish was granted soon.

43

'SEE, these two are not eating their food,'said Malti, complaining in a loving manner.

'Dadi, I am not hungry.'

'What happened? You did not eat last night too.'

Akanksha said, 'Dadi I am not hungry, how can I eat? I have a lot of work.'

'When have I stopped you? I haven't said anything to you.'

Akanksha, Aniruddh and Dadi's arguments were common in the house. Akanksha was growing up and turning stubborn with. Dadi, although illiterate, understood the temperament of the girl. Amit had observed that his mother's behaviour with Akanksha was now more like a friend than a grandmother. Akanksha was growing up to be a woman and the changes in her behaviour were noticed by grandmother. Nikita had no idea about anything, trapped as she was in her own world. Malti's behaviour with Aniruddh was different.

'Aniruddh, why haven't you had your milk?'

'Dadi, why are you after me?'

'Son, you will get weak. You have your cricket match tomorrow.'

'It's okay, I won't play.'

'What is the matter? Tell me or I will complain to your father.'

'Okay, tell him,' would be the immediate response from both kids. Amit was not a strict father—his own father had been a disciplinarian, but in a loving, kindly way.

After Malti's complaints, Amit would ask, 'What is the matter? What is the problem?'

'Papa, I am not hungry and Dadi is after my life,' complained Aniruddh who always talked like this about his grandmother.

'Ma, send them to the hospital. Let me get them checked and give them an injection each,' said Amit in a strict tone but with love in his eyes.

'Papa, don't joke,' they said in unison.

'When did I joke? You will be given an injection if you don't listen to your grandmother.'

Both the children loved their grandmother and considered it their right to fight with her. The room where Amit used to hear these fights had now fallen silent. Emptiness had invaded their lives.

44

AFTER Malti's death Amit felt an orphan. While she was alive, he was emotionally strong and was not worried about his children's welfare. Just seeing her face every day made him feel stronger. Now he needed love, knowing that physical love is as necessary as food and water, making negative energies like pain, anger, worry drain away when a man and a woman get intimate. The only woman in Amit's life had been Nikita. When Nikita would go off to sleep after having her medicines, Amit would gaze at her inert form, admiring her physical beauty. Sometimes Nikita wanted to make love to him, but his mental condition wouldn't allow Amit to let it happen at times. Even in moments of intimacy, Nikita would start acting strange and put off Amit.

One night, Nikita crossed all the limits. For the past two days, she had been troubling Akanksha. Amit was worrying about his daughter when Nikita came inside the room and stripped off her clothes. Then she said, 'Love me.' At that moment her naked body held no charm for Amit and he told her irritatedly, 'Have you no shame? Go to sleep. I am not in the mood.'

Nikita yelled, 'If you can't do it then say it...you can't make love to your woman and pretend to be a man. My life is ruined...I don't want to stay with an impotent man.' Nikita kept ranting and then went off to sleep.

This shook Amit up. He had to leave for night duty at the hospital which he'd taken up to stay away from Nikita. At least in the hospital he got a few hours of sleep and quiet. He quickly changed his clothes and thought, 'She is crazy.' He was late for the hospital but these words kept echoing in his head and in order to escape them he left without saying a word.

He knew he hadn't done anything wrong. Various ties bound him. He always thought about society and the family, not ever wanting to deviate from accepted norms, but sometimes the urge to have another women swamped him. He felt like going away somewhere—after all, he was human, not God. But the faces of his mother and Akanksha would flash in front of his eyes—now his daughter was a young woman and for him to go to a prostitute at his age was highly inappropriate. Such thoughts prevented him from taking any steps. Instead, to gain a few moments of happiness, he started drinking and would feel relieved for a while. He did not give a thought to whether drinking was good or bad for him, so long as his and his family's name was not tainted, he was fine. It was just the body which would get damaged, but whom did he have to live for? In times of extreme sadness he would drink and when he regained his senses, the worries about his children would prevent him from drinking for a few days.

That night, instead of the hospital, he went to a bar.

'What will you have?' asked the waiter handing him the menu card.

'One large whisky.'

'With soda or water?'

'Mixed.'

Amit felt very dejected. He did not want to think of what Nikita had said. Even knowing that her mental condition was responsible, it broke his heart. Nikita's words had wounded him deeply. He was unable to escape the words she had said. He downed his whisky. Having consulted a few psychiatrists, it was uncertain which mental disease she was suffering from. Some said it was schizophrenia, while others believed it to be bipolar disorder. The doctors had termed her condition as a psycho-affective disorder. Sometimes she would go into a depression and show signs of bipolar disorder and at other times, when getting angry at Akanksha, would show signs of schizophrenia. Amit knew that Nikita, in that mental framework, hated him and his family members. But her words tonight had disturbed him, whatever the nature of her disease.

He finished his first peg of whisky, the alcohol calming his brain.

'Sir, should I repeat the order?'

'Yes, bring another one.'

During his college days, on the insistence of his friends on Holi, he had taken his first drink. After that he used to enjoy a drink with his friends but now after marriage, he began to drink alone. He did not know whether it was good or bad for him but whatever came to the rescue was most welcome. Amit felt it was better to lose his balance than face reality; at least for a while he was happy in his own world. Drinking didn't always work and soon dark thoughts started crowding his mind.

'Sir, do you want any accompaniments?'

'No...okay get me a salad.... No, listen, get two boiled eggs.' After taking a peg, Amit felt hungry. He hadn't eaten properly. He felt the inherent need to be loved as the fumes of whisky began to cloud his mind. Tonight he had left home without even looking at his children nor had he asked whether they had eaten anything. What a life!

A ghazal about love was playing at the bar and he thought to himself...does real love happen in life?

The sip of whisky tasted sweet and he forgot Nikita's sharp tone and distant voice. Then he felt angry and took another sip of his third peg, which gave him some relief. Nikita's disease had no cure, it could only be kept at bay.

With the third peg, he needed a smoke. He lit a cigarette. Amit was in a trance and felt lightheaded. His mind was now befuddled as he gulped down his third peg. He paid the bill and went towards his car, opening the door with difficulty. He had no idea which gear the car was moving on. He reached the hospital on first gear.

45

It was ten in the night and the ward boy was asleep. The nurse was asleep in the duty room. Stumbling a little, he reached the doctor's duty room. He did not find Aditi there; it was her evening shift but she must have left. The door to the inner chamber was ajar and light softly fell inside. He went inside and stopped. Aditi was asleep, her sari a little displaced. Soft light fell on her body, defining the contours. His mind was out of control and he felt intensely attracted to her. He felt unstable and although he tried to stop himself he was helpless as he found himself moving towards Aditi. Amit knew he was drunk but the burning desire of his body engulfed him and he had to satisfy it. He reached Aditi, staring at her body and leaned towards her. He did not know what he was about to do but before he could touch her, her eyes flew open.

Aditi had faced all kinds of problems in her life. She never wanted anyone's support and in her quest for the purest form of love, she had accepted defeat. God had given her the strength to live independently, on her own terms. No man had dared to approach her because of her strong personality and the fear of being snubbed. She had heard footsteps in the room and saw Amit drunkenly staring at her—she could not believe her eyes. His hand was reaching out to touch her—it took her a second to understand but before he could touch her, she got up abruptly.

'When you are feeling better, we will talk.' Saying this she walked towards the door, turned, glared at him and left. The sharp noise of the door brought Amit back to his senses. Guilt pervaded his mind and heart.

46

ON one hand there was longing, suffering and pain and on the other, there was no peace. The thirst of the mind, soul and body had now started eating Amit up. He wished he would die but life went on. The only wish left was to see his children lead a normal life. He was worried about Akanksha, she was not at fault but he realized that all the women in his life had suffered—mother, sister, wife and now daughter. He had no desire left to live but what would happen to his children if he wasn't there? The thought scared him. But was he able to provide them with anything as long as he was alive? Nothing. Nikita remained mentally unstable—for a few days she would be all right but the effect on others by her bouts of rage would remain. Would Aditi be able to understand him? After what had happened, could he expect forgiveness from her? Maybe not... He felt close to Aditi, but why? After that night's incident he could not face her.

For Aditi, this was the most unexpected turn of events. She did not know much about his situation and living abroad had distanced her from him. She felt sad but she stopped herself from further investigating his condition. In the past few days, what Aditi saw and heard changed her perceptions. In order to rid Amit of his troubles, she could not ruin herself. For his desires, she could not trample her values. But yes, as a good friend, she would be there to share his troubles. Was it necessary to give such a relationship a name?

Her ties with Amit were old and she was with him out of friendship. Amit was again searching for support but this time it wasn't for himself. Amit had always told her everything about himself earlier and he had always got love, understanding and her trust. He kept debating whether or not to talk to her—he had no one else to go to apart from Aditi. Shyam and Radhika were there but he could not expect much from them. They had their own responsibilities and work to look after though he knew they would be ready to help him out. What would happen to the kids? What about Nikita?

Night turned to day. Aditi visited him in the hospital in the morning.

'I want to talk to you.' A soft voice reached Aditi's ears.

'Yes?' Aditi was surprised.

'I am ashamed of myself.'

'I understand everything now, you needn't say a thing.'

Amit lowered his eyes. Aditi took his hands in hers, seeing his eyes were brimming with tears. Aditi wiped his tears and said, 'You have to be strong...this cannot go on. I am with you.'

Aditi was sitting on a stool near his bed and noticed that the tears did not hide the extreme pain in his eyes. The morning light was trickling in through the glass panes of the window and the grey strands in his beard were telling their own story. Amit's situation had melted her heart and had given a new name to their relationship.

'That night the way I treated you, I hope you understand...' she said.

'I need you,' said Amit, without listening to her explanation.

Her grip loosened and she moved away from him and asked, 'What can I do for you?'

Amit looked at the ceiling for some time. He knew he had very little time and said, 'Save my daughter...she will be ruined.' He broke down and turned his face. Aditi sat shell-shocked and after some time lovingly put her hand on Amit's head. 'You will get better, nothing will happen to Akanksha.' She had no idea about Nikita's illness and thus, did not understand what was it that Amit feared or what could happen to Akanksha. She felt it was not appropriate to ask Amit in his condition.

After coming out of the room, she saw Akanksha running towards her with a thermos and a basket of food.

'Hello, Aunty, how is Papa?'

'He is all right. You didn't go to school?'

Shaking her head, she lowered her eyes. When Aditi tried to read Akanksha's face, she found an innocent and a sad girl with fatigue and pain in her eyes. At her age, girls enjoyed themselves, dressing up, enjoying life but she was, on the other hand, burdened with responsiblities. Aditi kissed Akanksha on her forehead and said, 'Your father is awake, let's go and have tea with him.'

Inside the room, Aditi sat on the sofa, Akanksha stood for two minutes looking at her father. The father and daughter exchanged looks, smiled, and she went to sit next to Aditi. Aditi observed Akanksha as she poured out tea and kept thinking about Amit's worry regarding her. Amit was content on seeing both of them together; it lightened the burden in his mind. Aditi sensed the immense amount of love the father and the daughter had for each other. It gave her a sense of the fatherly love she had never got.

Section 5

47

AMIT recovered and the doctors treating him said he could go back home. His children were delighted, but Amit had mixed feelings since he had to face the reality of life with Nikita again.

Knowing that Amit was worried about Akanksha, Aditi decided to find out a little about her life. She wanted to understand what was worrying Amit. So she went to Akanksha's school and asked her class teacher. 'She hardly attends school. She's irregular and not good at her school work,' said the teacher, who was Aditi's childhood friend. In two days, Aditi got to know about Akanksha looking after the house and being ill-treated by Nikita. Akanksha had not uttered a word about this and Amit was silent on the matter, but Aniruddh had told her a little bit when he saw his sister's closeness to Aditi. Aditi hardly got time to see Amit and was also looking after Amit's patients. Today she had got some time so she had visited the school. Thinking about what the teacher had told her, she crossed the State Bank and passing under the railway bridge, was going towards home. She was drawn to Akanksha. Maybe it was because of Amit's long-term friendship with her and his concern for Akanksha...or Akanksha's innocence and the emptiness in Aditi's life. At a crossing at Sadar, she saw Akanksha on a scooter with a boy. On hearing the car's honking, Akanksha turned to look, and when she saw Aditi, she seemed scared and said something to the boy. Aditi tried to catch up to have a better view of the boy. He was ordinary-looking, probably in his twenties. She did not like the way the boy had glared at her. Akanksha had tried to hide her face, fear reflected on it as if she had been caught stealing. Aditi understood the reason.

Akanksha got off the scooter a little distance from her home and

Aditi caught up with her, talked to her and brought her back to her place. Aditi did not ask her anything, but Akanksha began crying.

'Why are you crying? I haven't said anything to you. Don't worry, I will not tell your father or brother.' Aditi tried to win Akanksha's trust by hugging her. She did not want to discuss it any further, unless the girl wished to talk. Aditi heated up some food for Akanksha and while they ate, she asked, 'How do you go back home from school?'

'In a rickshaw.'

'And Aniruddh?'

'On a cycle.'

'On your way back home, you can drop in here whenever you feel like. I will be back home by two and we would love to have you around, don't you think so, Ma?' Aditi looked at her mother while asking this question. Sunita, who was usually bored alone at home, said, 'Please come to see your grandmother. I don't enjoy staying alone at home and if you visit, I will feel better. I regret making my daughter a doctor, she is hardly at home.' Sunita joked, looking at her daughter. Akanksha had got over her fear. They called Aniruddh, and later, when both of them were taking a stroll in the garden, they saw him at the gate on a cycle. After Aniruddh had had something to eat and both were about to leave, Aditi said, 'Akanksha, come straight here after school. Aniruddh can pick you up when his school hours are over.'

Akanksha began to follow the routine of going to Aditi's house after school and chatting with Sunita until Aditi came back. Sometimes Aniruddh would join them and all of them would enjoy a meal in the garden. Akanksha could not bring herself to talk about the boy but Aditi knew that the matter could be handled with love and trust.

She mentioned it to Amit who asked her, 'Since when has this been going on?'

'I don't know but I saw them on my way back home. I tried to find out about the boy—he lives in the outhouse.'

Lowering his eyes, he said, 'It is not Akanksha's fault. She was hardly looked after and never got her mother's love...' Aditi understood. Lack of money, poverty or food did not affect children as much as the lack of love. That was when a young person began to look for attention outside home. It wasn't the status of the boy that bothered Amit, it was the character and the intentions of the boy that worried him. Aditi knew this and her love and concern for Akanksha were evident to all including Sunita.

48

SUNITA had fallen very ill. Aditi hadn't gone to the hospital for the past few days so Amit paid her a visit at her place. Lying in bed, her face pale, she told Amit, 'I worry a lot about Aditi, she is all alone. I asked her to get married so many times. Initially she refused, but later asked me to search for someone for her, but I couldn't find anyone suitable.'

Amit pressed her hand and said reassuringly, 'Don't worry. I am there for her and so are my children.'

The next day, news came that Sunia had passed away.

All the doctors and the staff had gathered at Aditi's place to offer their condolences. Amit knew that now her loneliness would only intensify. Aniruddh and Akanksha could not contain their sorrow. Over the past few months, they had spent a great deal of time at Aditi's house and considered themselves part of the family. They had not dared to cry openly when Malti had passed away, fearing that it would bring on one of Nikita's fits of anger. The amount of love they had got from this house was beyond their expectation. They were free to fight, talk about their likes and dislikes and laugh. Aniruddh would tell Sunita about his favourite dishes a day before and the next day, it would be made. Sunita Dadi loved them and even if Aditi scolded them, they could feel her love. They both hugged Aditi and kept crying, knowing they had the freedom to express their sadness. Both of them expressed their grief to such an extent that Aditi had to calm them down.

Nikita was at home and was not even told about Sunita's death. The three of them had to lie to Nikita, not knowing how much their sadness would ruin her mood. By the time Amit returned to Aditi's place the next day, preparations for the last rites had been made. Sunita had no relatives, but her neighbours had arrived. Amit took the responsibility of organizing all the rites, remembering how Sunita had done a lot for him, how she had often fed him as a child when he was hungry. He wasn't trying to repay her for everything that she had done for him but was honouring the bond that had been created.

Aniruddh sobbed when he had to light the funeral pyre. After doing it, he sat down next to the pyre, holding his head in his hands.

Akanksha couldn't stop weeping. Aditi would take her in her arms and try to pacify her while at the same time kept wiping the tears that were welling up in her own eyes. It was a heart-wrenching scene to witness.

All the women of Darjani mohalla had come for the funeral, including Kamla. She was silent, unable to believe that the woman she used to criticize so severely was no more. All these women had attended Malti's funeral but Amit had been too busy handling Nikita. Her mental health had worsened at the time so he couldn't meet them. But on this day, as Aditi's friend, he had met everyone. Sethji's sons also attended the last rites. Their hatred for Sunita and Aditi had ended and they wanted to fulfill their father's last wish that they should look after Sunita.

Late in the evening, when everyone had left, Aditi looked bereft. Amit couln't see her in that state and left Akanksha with her.

When he returned home, Nikita asked him angrily where their daughter was. Where had they all gone? Then he told her, 'Sunita Aunty has passed away, I have left Akanksha at Aditi's house.'

Nikita did not say a word; Amit knew it was her low depression phase. In the morning she muttered, 'Tell her not to come back home. She must have confided in Aditi and Aditi must have told her everything about our college days. She dare not come back otherwise I will kill her.'

Akanksha stayed with Aditi for fifteen days and the bond between the two strengthened. There were purification rites, religious ceremonies and many visitors and Akanksha behaved like the daughter of the house, managing everything. When the time came for her to go back, she felt sad. She wondered whether the cooking and cleaning had been done back home. Aditi had asked her to go home; she did not want to be selfish and with a heavy heart, bid her goodbye.

When she reached home, Akanksha was scared so she stayed in her room and only later went to the kitchen. On hearing her movements in the kitchen, Nikita went there and found Akanksha. She erupted into a terrible fury that continued for a long time and Amit had to forcibly pull her away and make her take her medicines. Akanksha kept crying for several nights.

Aditi lapsed into apathy and even showed disinterest in the hospital. Amit knew that she was interested only in the children and always asked Amit about them.

49

'I need to talk to you,' said Aditi on the phone. Amit had just reached the hospital and said, 'Yes tell me.'

'Can you come to my room?'

Pausing for a few seconds, Amit said, 'Okay.'

Aditi had a calm look on her face. There was a long line of patients and the ward boy had been told to ask them to wait. Aditi asked, 'I want to ask you for something. Can you give it to me?'

Amit had no idea what Aditi wanted from him but he believed in her. He paused and asked, 'Why not?'

'I want your daughter,' said Aditi, looking straight into Amit's eyes. Amit saw hope as well as loneliness welling up in her eyes.

'I cannot live here any longer. I have no friends, no relatives. I know a lot of people in London and will easily get a job there. And I want to take your daughter with me. I have asked Akanksha but she will not go until you give her permission. This will be good for her considering the situation in your house. She will be my responsibility and I will get her admitted into any college at an undergraduate level, but I need your approval.' Aditi said this one breath and then continued, 'The other reason is that this society will not let me live. A single woman faces a lot of problems. I will not face these problems abroad. You must be wondering why I didn't get married, but I was too busy studying. Now I have to live alone—there will be questions. I am not afraid but I don't want to be trapped by them. Now when I have an opportunity, why shouldn't I make use of it? Our society raises all sorts of questions but has no answers. Hopefully, with time, answers will be given. As far as Akanksha's marriage is concerned, you start searching for a good match, but till then she will be my responsibility.' Aditi had chosen her words carefully. Amit had a right to refuse, but why would he do that? He would be sad to send his daughter away, but he knew life at home was hell for her. At least she could live a better life with Aditi.

'Okay, let me talk to her,' said Amit, getting up without looking at Aditi and left the room. In the afternoon, he had a talk with Akanksha. She said, 'I will do whatever you feel is right.' Amit knew his daughter well, that she wouldn't leave her parents without good reasons. Amit did not want to run away from his responsibilities but he knew he was unable to look after his children and was always under mental stress. Akanksha was getting motherly love from Aditi—what else could he wish for?

With a heavy heart, he agreed to Aditi's proposal and by the time Akanksha's first yearly exams had started, Aditi began making preparations. She was going to be bound in a relationship with a person who she would be responsible for.

Amit told Nikita, 'I am sending Akanksha abroad. She will no longer be a threat to you.' Nikita merely looked relieved.

That night when he went to the kids' room, both of them looked sad. Aniruddh kept quarrelling with Akanksha over small things, but she knew that this was her brother's way of expressing his love for her. After Aniruddh relaxed, she said in a mature fashion, 'You take care of Papa, and Papa, please take your medicines on time...both of you take care of Mom. Aniruddh, you will not fight with Mom and don't trouble Papa...I have told Lakshmi to make food every day.'

Amit listened to her and then asked, 'Are you happy?'

'Why wouldn't I be?...I have my father, mother, brother and now Aditi Aunty who loves me like a mother. I am going to live with her. I am not going forever, just for studies. Don't worry about me. She is with me,' said Akanksha wiping her tears.

Giving the title of 'Aunty' to Aditi forged a new relationship which Akanksha felt and Amit understood. There was now a new relationship between Amit and Aditi, which Akanksha had renewed. Any relationship is not possible without ties, they define relationships. All relationships are bound by them and it is these ties that define society and the family. Without these bonds, there would be no families or societies.

In the morning before leaving, Akanksha clung to her father and cried. Since her mother was asleep, she only touched her still feet.

Amit came back home after dropping Akanksha to Aditi's house. At home, he could feel Akanksha's presence in every corner. Aniruddh wept, but while Amit felt the loss acutely, he could not express it.

When Nikita got up, she searched for Akanksha and looked calm when she could not find her—but after some time, she grew silent. The depression phase had taken over and she remained silent for several days. What was going on in her head was difficult to understand but for days she did not mention Akanksha.

50

ANIRUDDH missed Akanksha a lot, she was not only his sister but his friend. At least she would be happy in her new surroundings and she was with Aditi Aunty, who would take good care of her.

A letter soon arrived from Akanksha. the last line was, 'I am happy, don't worry about me. I miss you.' There was a lot of pain in this line and he was filled with nostalgia. The house seemed haunted. At night, he gazed up at the high ceilings, feeling a void.

Nikita did not talk about Akanksha at all. He did not really understand her illness, but he wished his home was like his friends' where there was very little discord.

He remembered the Diwalis of his childhood when everyone else celebrated, but he was tense at home, listening to his mother's crying and yelling. As long as their grandmother was alive, they used to have a little bit of fun. She would make sweets for them and eating them secretly used to be fun. He would live for those moments. When his mother was feeling better, firecrackers would be bought but sometimes she would be terrified when they were lit. So they stopped that too, never knowing when her mood would change. Since his mother was not sociable, hardly any visitors turned up. He used to get angry thinking about how all their lives hinged on their mother's moods. Why couldn't they just let her sleep and get on with their own lives? This was the reason why he was angry with his father. He could not understand why the house revolved around his mother? Was she the centre? This kept him unhappy but when grandmother used to tell him stories about his father's childhood, he felt calmer. He and Akanksha used to sleep near their grandmother, which gave them a feeling of security. After her death, the house felt lonely and after Akanksha left, he couldn't bear to stay in that house. The whole night he would remember the old days. Living with his sister, he never felt alone because they would chat before falling asleep. He was scared of his mother's fits of madness, which could be triggered by the slightest spark, but living in fear wasn't the solution. That hurt him more and he felt like running away. It was because of Malti and then Akanksha that he hadn't escaped earlier.

He remembered that their grandmother called him Ani and Akanksha was called Akki.

He looked at her sister's empty bed, with its unwrinkled bedsheet. There were books on her table which lay unopened. In her letter, she had said that she was doing her graduation in History and English.

One night his loneliness increased to such an extent that he felt the house was going to eat him up. There were beads of sweat on his forehead. He couldn't disturb his father, who always worked too hard. He did not know when his loneliness got translated into fear. He got up and the darkness of the night started playing tricks on him. He felt a shadow creeping towards him, but when he switched on the light, there was no one there. He felt as if the shadow had entered him and wanted to run away from his own shadow. He took a deep breath. He was feeling thirsty but he could not go to the kitchen. The walls were plotting to kill him. Suddenly his attention got diverted to a photograph of Goddess Durga on the wall. His grandmother had told him to remember the goddess whenever he felt scared. He quickly stood in front of the photograph with folded hands and closed eyes. Slowly, he regained his composure and went off to sleep. Next morning he resolved to live with Aditi and his sister; he couldn't stay here. Papa and Mom could live the way they wanted to... Didn't he have a life of his own?

Aniruddh started working hard because he had an aim. His hard work paid off and he got admission at a medical college in London with the help of Aditi Aunty. Nikita was sad, but Amit explained, 'He is our son, if he won't study, what will he do? It's good that he is studying and will become a doctor like us.'

Amit knew he would miss him but, instead of being bound by love, it was better to sacrifice one's feeling for the happiness of a loved one.

51

ANIRUDDH had left home and even though Nikita was ill, she loved him. She realized that he wouldn't stay at home, he was grown up and wanted to give a new direction to his life. It was the month of February when the cold season was on its way out but the sun was still welcome. Nikita was sitting in an armchair with her eyes closed. Strands of her grey hair shone in the sunlight.

Amit had gone to drop Aniruddh to the station. There was a train from Jabalpur to Delhi and then a flight to London. Nikita was alone at home, a new lease of life was waiting for her. She had been freed of all her ties. Now all that was left was to wait. She did not know when she had fallen asleep. The cold air touched Nikita and made her comfortable. Amit returned from the station and on getting off the car was surprised to see Nikita in the garden with her eyes closed. Before she opened her eyes, Amit sat next to her and stroked her head lovingly. Nikita's mind was directionless. She opened her eyes and saw Amit looking at her. There was love in her eyes. The amount of yearning she felt for Aniruddh was evident. Amit continued to stroke her head.

Amit could not believe that Nikita had changed—the emptiness in her eyes was new. 'Do you want some tea?' asked Nikita, avoiding his eyes. Amit had been waiting to hear this for years. He stared at her, amazed, as Nikita went towards the kitchen. Had a new life begun?

But instead of going to the kitchen, Nikita turned and went back to her bedroom. The loneliness had started having its effect on her and she was lost in her world.

Amit kept sitting in their room for hours, feeling the chasm that his children's absence had left. Memories remained. He was happy with his decision to let them go, but missed them unbearably. He was afraid that he would never see them again.Would they be able to live without him?

Could he live without them? Everyone has to leave the parental home one day. Amit tried to look into his foggy memories—he had a hazy recollection of when they were born, when they grew up. He was extremely sad that he could not witness their childhood, could not be a part of it, preoccupied as he had been with Nikita. Now he would focus his attention once more on her.

Lakshmi had been a part of the house since Malti's time and was of great help. She was a kind woman and helped take care of Nikita. Amit used to call her up from the hospital to check on Nikita's condition. After that heart attack, Amit had given up smoking. Aditi and Akanksha had helped him kick the habit. Amit had followed their instructions. But whenever he was under a lot of stress, he would drink...he needed something at least!

52

BEING a doctor, Amit had some knowledge of mental illnesses and he had read several books and journals on this subject. He had slowly learned more about it and he knew that it was quite common now, to be found in every other house. But the difference lay in its intensity. There were several reasons for this disease—one was the stress of modern life and another was that it ran in the family. Not everyone inherits it from parents but the chances are high, a ten per cent possiblity to find it in a house with such a case history. It came in several forms—stress disorder, panic disorder and anxiety disorder. The common form of this disease was the thought disorder that Nikita suffered from. The biggest problem with this illness is that the patient is so wrapped up in his/her world that he/she feels perfectly normal, which is why the person does not want to see a doctor. Then, the social stigma attached to it prevents the family from taking the patient to a hospital. Due to lack of good hospitals, it is difficult to cure mental illness. Amit knew that it couldn't be cured but at least the quality of life could be improved. But in order to achieve that, time and help was required. He could not give enough time to Nikita and his children because of the various problems that cropped up. Nikita used to stay away from Malti and Akanksha while Aniruddh used to stay away from his mother. The environment of the house had been ruined but he had to do something. Amit found out that new and improved medicines had arrived in the market, so he decided to discuss this with Nikita and make her agree to take them.

Amit noticed that Nikita had a fear of people and was inclined to stay away from reality, drawn as she was into her own negative world. Apart from Aniruddh, for Nikita, other people—

Malti, Akanksha, Aditi and even Amit—were her enemies. Amit understood this and although he would get affected by her words at times, he had to overlook them. He still loved Nikita. He knew the symptoms—where there was a positive symptom and a negative symptom there was also a disorganized one and a distorted thought. In positive symptoms, there are positive as well as negative illusions. Amit observed that in Nikita's case, she suffered from the illusion that people were out there to kill her. In negative thoughts, she did not like meeting people. In disorganized and distorted thoughts, she would not think in the right direction and could not come to any logical conclusion. She would repeatedly make Amit wash his hands. She would take things only from the left hand and lacked confidence. When negative thoughts would increase, she would repeatedly make Malti wash her hands and curse Akanksha. Akanksha knew this, so she would give her tea with her left hand and repeatedly wash her hands. Nikita was only scared of Aniruddh, otherwise she lacked. After the death of Supriya and Malti, she never shed tears. For several days she went silent and kept herself locked in her room, lying on her bed covered with dirty bedsheets. Amit would have to sleep on it too, but got used to the smell.

Side-effects of anti-psychotic medicines like Haloperidol were bloating of her body and symptoms of Neuroleptic Malignant Syndrome (NMS), which made her muscles contract and cause pain. Her mouth would go dry, there would be pain in the stomach and difficult in passing urine, low blood pressure and shivering. Depression would set in and other systems would go haywire. Amit had heard about the new drug called Klonopin, to reduce these effects, but there were several other ways of treatment that Amit hadn't accepted.

One day he told Nikita, 'Look I have sent everyone away—Supriya, Ma and Akanksha. No one is out there to kill you and look, I have washed my hands.' Nikita calmed down listening to this and Amit would do whatever he could to humour and placate her. In this way, he gained her trust. She began sleeping like a child next to him. She would fall asleep and Amit would keep holding her in his arms, keeping the sense of touch alive. He had been physically close to this woman but now his ties with her were beyond those of physicality. Whenever he used to write to his children, he used to tell Nikita what he'd written and would sometimes read out their letters to her.

Nikita became calm and at times silently listened to whatever Amit told her. At times, when she was feeling better and Amit had to leave for hospital, she would bid him goodbye normally. At times she would talk to Lakshmi and even cook a little—and Amit ate everything she made, whether it was cooked well or not. Sometimes she would talk about her children for hours, worry about them and go off to sleep. She used to get disoriented often but the intensity was decreasing. Sometimes she sat in the garden, staring blankly at the sky even if Lakshmi called her. Amit kept the main gate locked so that she could not leave the house.

To keep his mind occupied, Amit took rounds of the hospital even when off duty and liked to chat with his patients. It gave him some contentment, but only after giving Nikita his time. If he had to go and buy groceries, he would take Nikita along. At times comical situations would arise like once she ordered two kilograms of salt and 100 grams of sugar. On being asked, she said, 'I have to run the house, you don't know a thing.' Even when people laughed at him, it did not affect him. It was his aim to keep Nikita occupied and instil confidence in her.

He could keep in touch with people from his neighbourhood because they visited the hospital for treatment. The older Mr Saini and Guptaji had passed away. Alka's mother, too, had passed away. He also got the news of Guruji's death and had gone to attend the last rites. Lallan had grown old but still sold milk. He had known Amit since childhood and loved him. He had expressed his concern regarding Nikita to Lakshmi. Sometimes he would sit on the steps of the bungalow and wouldn't leave till he had met Amit.

Amit was in touch with the leading psychiatrists, Dr Patel and

Dr Chaudhary and with the Bhusaval hospital's Dr Anand. On his advice, he decided to meet the famous psychiatrist, Dr Singh, in Himachal Pradesh. He would take Nikita with him and they could see the Himalayas and Shimla. He told Nikita only about the vacation to Shimla, saying that since the railway staff and administrators got free passes, he had got their bookings done. A guesthouse at Dharampur had been booked as well. There was a connecting train from Kalka to Shimla but Dr Singh's clinic was on the way to Dharampur. Amit and Nikita got off at Kalka and took a taxi for Dharampur. Dr Singh was famous for curing mental patients and that hope lead Amit to consult him.

When Nikita saw the mountains, she became as happy as a child. On the winding roads, Nikita got the car stopped, alighted and stood at the corner of the road. The ravines and the mountains surrounded them. The cold mountain wind was playing with her hair. After some time she asked, 'Have you brought me here to push me off the mountains?' For a minute he was perplexed and then laughed, 'No, you fool. We have come here on our honeymoon.'

Nikita looked happy, 'You never told me,' she smiled and kissed him. Then, in a shy manner, she said, 'This is one sweet honeymoon.'

Amit held her by her waist and looked into her eyes with love. He did not care about the world but yes, at that age, they were a sight to behold. The newly-wed honeymooners passing them by in their cars waved at them and the taxi driver was also smiling.

53

TIRED, Nikita fell asleep on reaching the guesthouse and Amit, without wasting any time, went to visit the doctor. The hospital was nearby. Dr Singh was an experienced man and said, 'Look Amit, being a doctor, you know the facts. One can get a lot of information on the internet, and a lot of research has been done on this kind of mental illness, but there is no complete cure for it. Yes, we can control it by making the patient symptom-free. Whatever symptom is seen in excess is checked and the patient can live normally. The side effects are very few. In fact, one out of five patients are cured enough to live normally. It all depends on the intensity, the condition of the patient and the medicines taken. Home, environment, age and other factors play an important role while healing the patient.'

Amit had read extensively on his but he nursed the hope of an ordinary man. If Nikita's condition could improve, why couldn't they try every possible treatment? The condition of the patient, the duration of the disease, the conditions at home, the method of treatment and the looking after of the patient—he could manage all of this, but would God be on their side? He was the One whose presence he had never felt. Amit was lost in his own thoughts and on seeing the number of patients he had asked, 'So many patients?'

'You are not the only one going through this. There are a lot of patients and only five per cent are able to reach us. Whoever turns up is treated at once and they do benefit. Today, because of the nuclear family, the stress of modern life, such numbers have increased. Earlier, the mother and wife used to be the pillars of strength and the men of the family used to come back home from work and be at ease. Now everywhere, there is confusion—fights at home, tension related to work, mental stress. Every home is dealing with its own set of problems. At times people are unable to understand the problems of others and such people get aggressive or cut themselves off from the world. They are unable to enjoy life and people brand them as, 'those always in a bad mood'. They call them erratic or in common language, depressed. When the condition reaches beyond handling then they are brought to doctors. You are lucky that you knew about this and started her treatment. There are people who don't understand the cause and suffer along with the patients.'

The doctor continued, 'The new world has given us new diseases for free. There are other reasons for it but loneliness has become the main reason.' The doctor would have continued but was interrupted by a nurse who said, 'Sir, an old patient has hurt her head and wants to see you.'

'Send her here.'

The moment she entered, there was bedlam. She screamed, 'I can't live with this bastard—see, he beat me up! See the blood!' The man with her was silent. There was a young man and his wife behind them, who looked sad.

'Don't worry, we will look into the matter. You go to your room. I am coming.' Instructing the nurse to give her a tranquillizer, he sent her out of the room. The man pleaded with folded hands, 'What to do? She created a storm. When all of us were coming here, she attacked her daughter-in-law. I had to beat her otherwise she would have killed her.'

The family looked intensely worried as the doctor instructed the nurse to prepare a room for electric shock treatment and told the family to stay away.

'Look at this case. The man loves his wife and is loved in return when the woman is in a better condition but at times she considers him to be her worst enemy. Still, the man has looked after her for the past twenty-five years and gets beaten up at times as well.'

'But, Doctor, electric shock?'

'I think it is important. Some doctors are against it but, in a country like India where facilities are few, this is the best option. I am speaking from experience when I say this treatment is effective. Nothing in this world is perfect and in my life I have never seen more permanent memory loss than this one—yes, it does affect the temprorary memory, but with some patients it is necessary.'

Saying this, the doctor left to attend to the patient and Amit, on coming out of the room, was lost in the sea of patients. He saw the man standing outside the room where the electric shock was being given. Amit felt like talking to him so he went up to him and asked him about his situation.

The man warmed up to him and said, 'Since the time she has come to my house, I have had a difficult life.'

'How many years have you two been together? Do you have kids?'

'As long as she was fine we had kids but I have dedicated my whole life to her... I am half-dead but I cannot abandon her...she is my wife!'

The meaning of relationships, strength of ties and the sacrifice involved made Amit feel that, maybe, it wasn't all bad. Nikita had given him two kids and so much love—he felt like a new direction had been given to him.

When he reached the guest house, he saw Nikita in a black sleeveless gown, the colour accentuating her fairness. The deep neck was showing the beauty of her bosom. The effect of medicines and the tiredness on her face was apparent. Her hair hung loose and the silver strands only enhanced her beauty. She hugged him and said softly, 'It's our honeymoon...' Lowering her eyes, she whispered, 'Love me.' After what seemed like a lifetime, he took off his clothes, clasped her in his arms and kissed her face. He kept playing with her body and Nikita, in a shy manner, kept telling him where to touch her. The entire night passed in a haze and in the morning they got up really late. There was a sparkle in Nikita's eyes and happiness on Amit's face. They spent their day in Kasauli and since they were leaving the next day, he took Nikita to Dr Singh's house in the evening. He had heard about the medicines Dr Singh had prescribed, saying that they were to be taken for two to three months. He added, 'The side effects are negligible.'

Nikita was taking a stroll in the garden and Dr Singh, on seeing her, said, 'You are lucky...she is beautiful.'

After hearing the doctor's advice, Amit and Nikita left for Shimla. He was impressed by the doctor's way of accepting a person the way he/she was and finding good qualities in them. The weather was pleasant in Shimla. He had heard about the Mall Road and wanted to visit it. Nikita grew excited and tried dressing up. She looked pretty in saris and today she chose a light blue one, which she struggled to wear. When she was applying make-up, she messed it up and by the time she was ready, she looked like an actor from a drama company. Amit kept observing her for an hour and before they were leaving, she looked at herself in the mirror and put on lipstick. Amit kissed her on her forehead and they went to the Mall Road. The evening wind was cold and she wrapped her shawl around herself. There were other couples, too, who were taking a stroll, holding hands. Nikita and Amit held hands, walking closely to each other and enjoying the physical closeness.

'I wanted to give you a honeymoon gift. Although it was supposed to be a surprise. Tell me what you want.'

'I want a sari,' said Nikita slowly, firmly holding his hand.

'Yes, why not?'

There were many couples at a shop buying suits and saris. Nikita was happy to see them and on overhearing one of them, Nikita said, 'I want to buy a sari for my mother-in-law...a lovely one and a suit for my sister-in-law.'

Amit was confused but not wanting to remind her that the two were long gone, he said, 'I don't want to give Ma an expensive sari. She is old so where will she wear such a sari in a small town? Supriya dirties her clothes so no point buying expensive things.' Amit smiled and helped Nikita to buy an expensive sari for herself.

After shopping when they came out, Nikita had a blank expression on her face. Till eleven she sat with him at the Ridge staring at the stars and the flickering lights on the mountainside. Amit was feeling very cold and he was shivering, but he knew this sudden trembling was not only because of the icy air. Nikita did not seem to feel the cold and remained expressionless.

On the way back, Nikita remembered Akanksha and began to curse her.

54

As time passed, Amit grew weaker. He knew Nikita couldn't be cured but what would happen after this? He constantly worried about this. One day a call came from Delhi. It was about Pranita, Nikita's twin sister, beautiful and attractive like her but very quiet. Whatever love he had got from that family had been from Pranita. She had married into a business family. Forgetting all the past insults, Amit had attended the wedding with Nikita but had returned on the wedding night after he felt insulted by the way the family treated him, as if he were an inferior being. Nikita's parents wanted her to get married into a rich family because money was what mattered the most to them.

That day, Mrs Sood, his mother-in-law, was on the line crying.

'What happened?' he asked.

'Pranita's husband has filed for a divorce and she is very depressed'.

'But I thought they were quite happy.'

'Yes, but for the past few months, she started behaving strangely. My son-in-law said that he did not want to spend his life with a maniac—we tried to make him understand but he wouldn't. He wants nothing to do with her and has taken the kids away as well.'

'Tell me, what can I do for you?'

'Call Pranita over for a few days. Her father is unwell and hasn't eaten or drunk anything for the past seven days. He had to be admitted to the hospital. My son does not want to keep his sister at home because my daughter-in-law threatens to leave home if she even enters the house.'

'What happened to Nikita's father?'

'I won't hide it from you...he has been suffering from

depression. I want him to get well and have been taking him to the hospital, getting him treated. Sometimes he gets angry and starts fighting...you know how it is—the bipolar disorder. After hearing about Pranita, he went into a psychotic state and...' Mrs Sood broke down on the telephone.

Amit was stunned. Strange are the ways of the world. In his eyes, Pranita had been happy with her husband and his family. Nikita could not stop gushing about her family and how there was a lot of respect for that rich son-in-law. And when he had told the family about Nikita, all they had said was, 'You want to leave her? Are you collecting evidence for a divorce?'

After that, he had not gone back to visit them and had taken a vow never to meet them. But now he softened.

'Let me talk to Nikita, she is unwell too. Don't worry, something will work out.'

Amit told Nikita, 'Let's invite Pranita over. It's just a matter of few days and we should help people in need.'

Nikita said, 'No, I refuse. We haven't taken up the responsibility for other people. Pranita is smart, she doesn't listen to my parents and keeps telling them not to interfere in our matters. I always listen to Ma and that is why I am happy. Ma always told us that in-laws are bad and that is true. I killed everybody here but no one could kill me. Pranita never listened to her and see how bad her in-laws are; they've left her to die. I don't want anyone staying in my house. How can I trust her?'

Amit did not know what to say. Had Nikita's mother actually said such things? Then he thought about what the doctor had said—mental illness could run in the family. Pranita was also mentally ill but the difference lay in the fact that the intensity was less and her condition started late. Amit felt helpless.

55

AT the children's insistence, Amit bought a computer and installed an internet connection. Now he could email them and stay in touch. Aditi used to email him as well. She felt it her duty to keep him informed. Akanksha had completed her graduation from Oxford University in history and English. She had once written to her father, 'Man never learns from history and that is why mistakes keep repeating themselves. The victorious have given history their version. Every language has a history and history has an influence on language. It is influenced by the grammar of a language. Every language has had its own history of progress, why haven't human beings learnt from it?' England was very conducive for such research. Akanksha wanted to go ahead with her studies but Amit wanted to meet them—it had been years since he had seen them. Even Nikita used to cry when she missed Aniruddh.

Then, one day, both of them came back to Jabalpur with Aditi. Aniruddh stayed at home but Akanksha and Aditi took a hotel room. Akanksha had grown up to be a beautiful woman but still retained her innocence.

She said, 'Aunty, Papa hasn't been taking care of himself. He has become so weak!' She scolded her father for some time, in angry words spoken with love. Later, Aditi said the same thing, 'Why don't you take care of yourself?'

'Now I have no worries. You are there to take care of the children.'

Amit smiled at her and after remaining silent for some time said, 'Akanksha has grown up and we need to think about her marriage. This is my last wish.' His voice sounded serious and Aditi felt the gravity of what he was saying.

'Okay, I'll talk to her and you start searching for a suitable match,' said Aditi.

'How is Aniruddh doing?'

'Now he is much better, otherwise...' Aditi tried to change the topic.

'Otherwise?'

Amit had lines of worry on his forehead that deepened.

'Nothing...he studies a lot, doesn't take care of himself. Now he is fine.' Aditi cleverly changed the topic.

Those fifteen days seemed like a blur. Once, when visiting home, Akanksha saw her mother asleep and wanted to meet her badly but couldn't because Amit thought it best that she keep away from Nikita. She cried a lot and wanted them to visit London. 'Bring Mom along too.'

'Yes I will.'

Amit did not know how to thank Aditi for giving his children a better life.

After the kids left, Amit was saddened. He took Nikita with him on a vacation to South India so that he could keep his mind off the children. They kept sitting for hours, watching the waves pounding the sand on the beach. Nikita was extremely quiet, it was the effect of the medicines. Her symptoms of anger had decreased and the new medicines had less side-effects. Amit, although only fifty years old, looked much older than his years and now his mind was fixed on one aim—he was waiting for Akanksha to get married.

56

AMIT had sent proposals to several families for Akanksha. He kept searching on the internet for suitable alliances but had no luck. Sometimes the boy was not capable enough, sometimes the family was not right. He had no relatives to help him and it was so difficult to get an arranged marriage proposal in this day and age for a boy or a girl. At times, people used to back out after hearing about Nikita's mental health, Amit was angry and worried at the same time. Society had created problems but provided no solutions.

One family liked Akanksha's photograph. The boy was working in an MNC—the company was based in England. Amit briefed them about Nikita's mental status, certain that it would be unwise not to tell the truth. In spite of this, the family had given their approval for marriage.

Once the boy's mother had called up when Amit was not at home. Nikita had received the call and she wouldn't stop saying, 'Akanksha is not my child…if you don't believe me, ask the people in the college.' The boy's mother tried to calm her but Nikita kept talking wildly. The boy's family decided to call the marriage off.

By the time Amit got to know what had happened, the situation was beyond repair. He tried to make the family understand but they wouldn't. The boy's father had the final word, saying, 'One doesn't drink milk that has a fly in it. If the girl's mother has such a mindset, what more can we say?'

Amit said angrily to Nikita, 'She is my daughter, not yours. I accept that. But don't you dare say anything like that again.'

Nikita was quiet like a child but her eyes were brimming with satisfaction. 'She resembles you...she is your child...not mine.'

Hearing this, Amit gave up.

Amit communciated the entire matter to Aditi through email. And as always, Aditi told him not to worry.

After coming back from India, Aditi had discussed the topic of marriage with Akanksha. She wanted it to be an open, frank conversation, so she asked her, 'Are you interested in anyone? Have you met anyone you would like to marry?'

Aditi wanted her to speak out but she refused. Even for her closest friend, Matthew, she had nothing to say. Matthew was her British friend, an intelligent and a calm person.

Aditi did not get to hear about any feelings that Akanksha had for anyone. When Akanksha said she didn't want to get married, Aditi tried to make her understand, 'Marriage is an important relationship between a man and a woman. It is the cornerstone of a family and society. There is excitement when one is free but happiness and contentment is to be found in ties. Without ties and sacrifice, love cannot be called love.'

Akanksha listened to Aditi silently. She continued, 'Studies are important but to have only a career comes at a cost. If there is no happiness in one's life then everything is meaningless. How long can one live alone? To live for someone else is a pleasure. A woman is complete when she becomes a mother. The origin of this world lies in pain and only a woman can bear it. The woman is the centre of the family and society. It is the way nature works and trying to go against it is foolishness. If a woman shows her love, a man would never break his ties. You have nurtured so many bonds—as a granddaughter, a daughter, a sister and you don't want to feel the happiness motherhood brings? Look at it this way, if you two were not there, what would my life be like?'

Akanksha lowered her eyes.

'I attained everything that I wanted but could never become a wife and a mother. By the time I understood the importance of marriage, I was past that age.'

'And what am I to you, Aunty?'

'You are my lovely daughter.'

'Then you are my mother,' Akanksha hugged her and said, 'I will never leave you.'

'No, you should be happy in your home, with your own husband and children. Whenever you want to meet me, I will be there. You have that freedom and that right.'

In the end, Akanksha accepted Aditi's advice.

57

ANIRUDDH often felt scared at night. He would feel that someone was following him to the steps of the hostel. On the tube, in the bus, he would often feel as if a spectre wanted to absorb him into its shadow. If he met a policeman on the way, he would feel that he had done something wrong and actually begin behaving in a suspicious manner. Everything scared him these days. Riddled with doubts, he was losing his confidence and negative thoughts surrounded him.

Once, in his hostel room, he got so worried by the shadows surrounding him threateningly that he was unable to sleep. Even the sound of the clock ticking was bothering him in the silence. Sometimes he would lie on the bed, at times sit on the floor, hiding his face as he leant against the wall. He could not gather the courage to go to the bathroom and beads of sweat trickled down to his trembling lips. Finally, he called up Aditi at five in the morning. Akanksha picked up the phone and Aniruddh said, 'I want to talk to Aditi Aunty.'

'Why, won't you speak to me first?'

'Ah, yes...yes,' Aniruddh sounded scared.

'What has happened?' Akanksha was extremely worried. Aditi woke up hearing her voice and taking the phone from Akanksha, said, 'What happened, son?'

'Aunty, I am very scared, please come,' said Aniruddh.

'But what has happened?' asked Aditi.

Aniruddh started crying and said, 'I get very scared at night...I feel something terrible will happen to me.'

'I am coming, don't worry.'

Without wasting any time, Aditi changed her clothes and

told Akanksha to come later by the tube. She left for London immediately in her car. It took an hour to Paddington and an hour and fifteen minutes to Birmingham by train, but she did not want to waste time asking about bus or train timings. Every minute was precious. She found a clear road on reaching Oxford City Centre Cross and turned onto the M40 motorway. She had decided that she would turn onto the M25 on reaching London.

Since there was less traffic on the M40, her mind was clear now and she could concentrate on the problem. Suddenly, the thought struck her, 'Has Aniruddh inherited Nikita's illness?' At that moment, she pressed hard on the accelerator and before the car got out of control, she put a stop to all her thoughts by saying a vehement 'No'. She tried to think calmly—no, she would not let this happen to him. She crossed the speed limit on several occasions and because of this, she reached in record time.

On reaching the hostel, she ran up the stairs and rushed to Aniruddh's room. There she held him in her arms and calmed him down. She kept stroking his forehead and kissing him affectionately. When he was feeling a little better, she sat next to him, talking to him. He told her of the chilling terror he'd felt and then his other small fears, like the strange feeling that he had put down the wrong roll number after giving an exam.

Aditi was a doctor. She had read up on mental illnesses in order to help Amit. On listening to Aniruddh, she realized that this was the beginning of a psychiatric disorder and began to worry about him. But she did not express her anxiety to him. By the time Akanksha arrived, she had settled his room and was talking to him as if nothing had happened.

When Aditi and Akanksha went back to Oxford, Aditi controlled her own emotions and slowly broke the news to Akanksha. She knew that Akanksha would be shattered to hear this. However, Akanksha handled it well and expressed her desire to do whatever it took to help Aniruddh out of this.

Aditi consulted a doctor soon and they shifted from Oxford

to London. Aniruddh was made to shift from the hostel to the house. Without talking to him much about it, she ensured he was always kept busy with work. Efforts were made to maintain a positive atmosphere around him and to build his self-confidence. They were trying to prepare him to face the reality. Aditi would not leave him alone even for a minute and took care of his likes and dislikes. Every day, they would go for long runs and during a holiday, they would go for long drives or go for a game or movies. There were always festivities at home. Even if Aditi would scold Aniruddh for something, she would show him a lot of affection as well. They had to be careful to not let any negative thoughts breed in his mind.

Akanksha would be with her brother at all times and Aditi would talk to him for hours when he came back from college. She was more like a friend to him. She had taken leave from her work to spend time with him.

Aniruddh felt happy and content with Aditi and Akanksha. Always enthusiastic about doing new things, his fear was going away. His confidence had defeated the negative thoughts and won over his fears. He was now ready to face life and its realities.

Aditi did not mention Aniruddh's brush with mental illness to anyone and kept it from Amit and even Aniruddh. That is why, on her trip to India, when Amit asked her about Aniruddh, she had remained quiet.

Aditi minutely observed Aniruddh while talking to him. She would consult the leading doctors of London's psychiatric institute when he went to college. She had started reading up on and following various therapies like talking therapy, behaviour therapy and psycho-dynamic therapy. She even made Aniruddh start with meditation and sometimes all three of them would meditate together.

Aditi felt that if she failed in treating the boy she considered her son, despite being a doctor, then all her training was a waste. She did not have much faith in God, but at times she used to thank

Him for the fact that she got to know of the disease at an early stage and got the chance to stop it from getting worse.

In the end, her efforts paid off and Aniruddh recovered.

Aniruddh was proud of and loved his aunt and sister. He had realized by now that he had escaped entering a dark and treacherous path. However, he had seen the turn into that path and at times the worry became evident in his eyes, but his will power and self-confidence had defeated it.

On Aditi's advice, meditation had become a part of his daily routine and yoga kept him healthy. He had started seeing life in a positive way, thanks to her. He accepted life's battles and was not afraid of failure nor was he jealous of others' achievements. Life was meant to be lived, not just spent somehow. One had to accept it the way one received it. After going through this phase, he understood his mother's condition and felt sorry for her. He was filled with love and pride for his father and appreciated him for handling his mother's illness with such courage.

Aditi knew several of Aniruddh's senior professors. She often spoke to them about him. Later, she started working in the same hospital as him and did not leave him alone even at home.

One day, after returning from India, Aniruddh told Aditi, 'I want to specialize in psychotherapy. I will be happy if I can do something in this field. Having been through this myself, I realize what a patient goes through and can understand a person's problems better.'

Aditi was very happy to hear this. She wanted Aniruddh to be confident about himself, and she didn't see any problem with his choice of specialization. One who has experienced darkness understands it better and knows how to dispel it; and Aniruddh had now walked into the light.

58

'EVEN though we live in Delhi, we hardly meet each other. I thought this was a good opportunity to meet you both. I am collecting money for our college's golden jubilee function. So, how is life?' Vikram had gone to visit Shyam and Radhika at their place. Both of them did not want to meet him but one cannot drive a guest away. Living in Delhi, Shyam and Radhika knew all about Vikram's life, they often heard about him but chose to be strangers to him.

Shyam replied very simply, 'Nothing much, yaar, just didn't find the time. So, how is life treating you?'

'Life is perfect, no tension. Only fun.'

Radhika served him tea and snacks reluctantly.

'So, who else are you guys in touch with from our batch?' Vikram was trying to take the conversation further.

Shyam knew that Vikram was asking this question to find out about Amit and Nikita.

'We keep talking to several of them,' Shyam replied dryly.

'So, how many kids do you have?' asked Radhika.

Vikram laughed and said, 'I don't want to be tied down, I want to live my life and enjoy it. I haven't really settled down yet. Haven't even thought about kids.'

Shyam knew that Vikram had had three unsuccessful marriages.

'Vikram, you must have got everything except love. And it seems you won't get that ever. For, love demands a certain commitment and you don't want to be tied down by any relationship,' saying this Radhika went inside the room.

Surprised at Radhika's comment, Vikram couldn't say anything further and left soon.

The year 2004–05 was the golden jublilee year for the Jabalpur Medical College. If one went through the pages of history, one would find that the college was established in 1955.

Amit, too, had started visiting the college again due to his involvement with a few programmes for the golden jubilee. He was not participating very actively but new information about the college interested him. Shyam, Radhika and Rajesh were coming for the celebrations with their families but Aditi was unable to come all the way from London.

Amit was surprised to know that the college had started with only twenty-five students as the Government Science College in Pachpedi, Jabalpur. The classes for clinical studies were conducted in the Seth Govind Das Hospital, which was earlier known as Victoria Hospital. He did not know all this about the college even when he was studying there! He was delighted to find out that Pandit Jawaharlal Nehru had laid the foundation stone of his college in 1959 and the college building had come up in the next five years. The college had progressed very well in the past fifty years. Now, around 750 undergraduates and 150 postgraduates received their degrees from seventeen departments every year. The paramedical department had also started offering two degree, two certificate and six-month diploma courses in the intervening years. Nikita would also listen to all this information with interest when Amit narrated these to her with excitement.

Preparations were on at full swing in the college. The Jabalpur Medical College of their times was called Netaji Subhash Chandra Medical College since 1997. Some of the professors from their time were still teaching there while others, though retired, still held consulting positions. All the old doctors were very happy to meet Amit. He met his old college friends and discussed things with them through the phone and internet.

Amit was remembering his college days. He had stayed in the hostel with Shyam on several occasions and had been ragged here. Taking a walk in the Takshashila, Royal and Prince hostels, he renewed his memories. The buildings were in a bad condition and there were plans to renovate them over the coming year. The visit to the the girls' hostel transported him to the palace of his dreams. Time changes everything...Nikita's beautiful face and lively eyes flashed in front of him.

After becoming autonomous, the college had undergone several changes. New machines, new labs and new departments had been set up. A new ICU with a modern central monitoring system had been set up. All the eight operation theatres had been improved and now the dean's office was being renovated.

Amit had to go to the college to attend the meeting of the chief committee and had taken Nikita along. She was much better now. There was a certain calmness about her now and it seemed that she was coming to terms with life's truths. On her way to the college, she kept looking at all arrangements for the Navdurga festival. She stood in front of the college for hours and then kept strolling near the hostel.

There was a stillness on her face when she returned. On their way back, while sitting in the car, she said, without looking at Amit, 'This life was wasted. Maybe it was all my fault.'

The quietness on her face was turning into sadness. The truth of life is to accept reality. Amit felt that the fact that Nikita was saying this was a sign that she was improving.

Night had fallen. Before reaching home, Nikita said, piercing the sadness, 'Vikram was right and so was everyone else in laughing at me.'

Amit felt that he hadn't heard her words correctly.

As soon as they reached home, Nikita went to bed without changing her clothes. She kept looking at Amit for some time and said staring into nothingness, 'You killed my child...you created the distance between me and Vikram to get me. Vikram would not have gone if you hadn't come. Why did you come to me?'

Changing into his pyjamas, Amit lay on the bed. He had no answer to her words. Since when did Nikita harbour such thoughts and why? Was this the reason she made him wash his hands repeatedly? Maybe she never loved him but didn't she even think of him as her support? Even if he accepted this, did she actually accuse him of being her child's murderer? Her last words had wounded him deeply. In a state of shock he forgot that Nikita was mentally ill and her thoughts were disturbed. He felt completely defeated and lay facing the wall beyond which he could see nothing. He didn't realize when his eyes fell shut.

59

At London's Heathrow Airport, Aditi was sitting with Akanksha and Aniruddh, waiting for the boarding announcement. Matthew was with them. All of them had been planning to go to India but none of them had imagined that it would be so soon. Besides, it is not necessary that all the plans one makes will see the light of day. But why did this happen with her all the time? She had waited so many times at this airport...in a different condition each time... Suddenly, her eyes pierced the crowd and she felt as if everybody had fallen silent. There was the silence of death all around.

No, these were just her thoughts...and she looked at Akanksha. A glance at her face showed that she had been crying for days and now her tears had dried up. She was sitting with her head resting on Aditi's shoulder. Pain was evident on her face and her mind was tired. It was difficult to come to terms with the fact that people could go so far away that meeting them again was an impossibility.

Akanksha felt like crying again. Even when she was leaving India for England, she had a feeling that she was going very far away. When would she meet her parents again? But now she could not stop her tears. Matthew would look at her every now and then and stroke her forehead. Seeing her suffer was painful for him too. Aniruddh was in a wretched state. He had not trimmed his beard for days. He had to perform his duties as a son but now he had duties towards his sister too, and this had broken him down.

Aditi looked at her watch again. She was aware of her responsibilities and wanted to reach India soon. They were already late. To begin with, there were the issues of visa and bookings and moreover, Akanksha had gone into a state of shock after hearing about her father and had to be admitted to a hospital. Matthew had stayed with her and looked after her in the hospital. Aditi was happy to see his attachment to her and this had taken away some of her worries.

They were on their way to India because Amit was dead.

Akanksha had made the right choice; Matthew loved her a lot and this is what mattered in a life partner irrespective of which country and which religion he belonged to.

Matthew used to refer to Aditi as Aunt, but Akanksha dissuaded him from doing so and asked him to call her 'Masi'. He was confused and did not understand the significance of this word and these relationships. 'A Masi is not a mother but she is like one,' she had tried to explain to him but how could he have understood something that he had no idea about? Once, he even said jokingly, 'Then she must be your father's second wife.'

Akanksha had replied angrily, 'No.'

Akanksha told Aditi about this conversation and Aditi laughed. Matthew was very nervous when he came home for the first time. Akanksha had told him that her aunt's decision was the final one. On coming home, he was swept away by Aditi's love and realized the importance of the relationship between her and Akanksha. He was amazed to see and experience this relationship of love which didn't have a name. He was intoxicated by it, as if he'd downed a glass of wine. Before leaving, he had touched her feet and won Aditi's heart.

Aditi had put a few restrictions on them and ground rules before they got married. Both Matthew and Akanksha were mature adults; they understood and complied with her request. Aditi wanted them to meet Amit once, but an email had changed everything. A call from India confirming the news had destroyed Akanksha's and Aniruddh's world.

60

THE Navratras had begun. Amit hadn't woken up and it was late in the morning. Lallan had come to deliver milk and was surprised to see Nikita coming out with the utensil to take milk. She said anxiously, 'Lallan ji, Amit isn't waking up today. Could you please see what is the matter?'

Lallan stared at her. Her voice was calm, face slightly swollen and hair dishevelled. The premonition of a mishap had brought him on the verge of tears. Hesitant to enter the house on his own, he called out to Lakshmi. Nikita stood close by, looking at them. Both of them went inside and found Amit lying on the bed with his eyes wide open. It seemed as if he was waiting for someone. They shook him but his body was lifeless and there was no response. Lallan broke into tears and Lakshmi, too, couldn't stop the stream of tears from her eyes.

Nikita stood like a stone at the door and said innocently, 'I checked but could not find Doctor Sahib's pulse.' Today, the blankness in her eyes was replaced by sadness and now they were drowning in sleep.

Lallan ran outside and gathered people. Everyone had arrived by afternoon. They tried to get Nikita to sleep but she would get up at frequent intervals and ask, 'What has happened?'

The people from Darjani mohalla had arrived. Aditi had called from London to enquire about what had happened as the children had received a strange email which did not make any sense. Aditi got to know about Amit's death through that phone call. Since it wasn't possible for the children to come back in time, the cremation had been done. Later in the evening, Nikita got up and asked, 'Where is the doctor? I had informed them through email...haven't they arrived?'

They tried to calm her but she kept insisting, 'I have some work with Amit...I have to meet him.'

The entire responsibility of the house was now on the neighbourhood; they had to wait for the children to return. 'We will definitely be there before the thirteenth day,' Aditi had said on the phone. 'Akanksha fainted on hearing the news and is in the hospital; we will be there earlier if she recovers before that.'

The Dussehra celebrations were dampened; the house that had remained closed for some time had been completely destroyed now. They had never imagined that somebody's grief could have an end like this. There was sadness everywhere. There was no enthusiasm or excitement during the evening aarti any more, there was just one question in everyone's eyes for the goddess, 'What kind of justice is this?'

One day, Nikita reached Darjani mohalla, with Lallan's help. She had begged him to take her there because she had to find Amit. She said frantically, 'Amit would be here.' She went around the neighbourhood asking for him in each house. She knocked at each door, scratched her head and asked, 'Is Amit here?'

She kept knocking at all the doors for a long time. When she knocked at the door of Amit's old house, a young man led her away from there saying, 'No one lives here any more.'

Nikita turned and looked at that door several times—some memories were coming back to her but her mind would get clouded again. This carried on till evening. When she could not find Amit, she went to the mandap and started asking a group of children, 'Beta, have you seen Amit Uncle?'

One child replied innocently, 'Amit Uncle has gone to meet his mother.'

On hearing this, Nikita kept sitting inside the Durga mandap waiting for Amit. Several women saw her in this state and broke into tears, thinking, 'At least she is sitting in the goddess' durbar.' Lallan could only look on helplessly.

Aditi wanted to reach home as soon as possible. It was the

thirteenth day after Amit's death. On landing at the Delhi airport, they booked train tickets for Jabalpur. It was unfortunate that there were no flights to Jabalpur. The train was running late and Aditi was worried as she wanted the children to at least attend the ceremonies on the thirteenth day. Aniruddh was worried about his mother while Akanksha hadn't recovered yet.

Although an hour late, the train arrived at Jabalpur around seven in the morning and they took an auto for the railway bungalow. Even though the house was close to the station, it seemed to be far away today.

On reaching, they saw that a crowd had gathered outside the house. Aniruddh jumped from the auto and ran towards the house while Aditi followed him. What they saw left them shocked. Aniruddh called out for his sister. Akanksha came running along with Matthew. She almost fainted on seeing what lay ahead. On the road was the corpse of her mother covered in blood. She had died when she ran out on the road to find Amit, not seeing the car that hurtled towards her. She had died instantly. The police had arrived earlier and had recovered a note in her hand that said, 'Aniruddh, I am going in search of your father. Don't tell Akanksha. His hands are very dirty and I have to get them cleaned. If you find him, let me know.'

Akanksha steeled herself. She sat on the road and kissed her mother's face repeatedly. Some of the blood was now on her hands and face and her tears were attempting to wash it away.

Matthew had finally met Akanksha's mother and was praying for her. He could feel a strong unbreakable bond being created. Standing behind the two children was Aditi, who had placed her hands gently on their heads. She had once again succeeded in controlling her tears.

Late in the evening, Aniruddh performed his mother's last rites on the same spot where his father's last rites had been conducted thirteen days earlier. Looking at the flames he thought,

'Father couldn't free himself from the bond with mother and neither could she...'